THE
DEVIL'S
PAWN

THE
DEVIL'S
PAWN

MARILYN LEVINSON

Author Photo Credit: Elizabeth Kilion

Second edition

ISBN: 978-1-68512-579-0

Cover art by Level Best Designs

This book was professionally typeset on Reedsy.
Find out more at reedsy.com

For Socrates, my long-ago first love and now my dear friend.

Chapter One

I'd almost made it to the front door when my uncle called to me. "Gregory, do you have a minute?"

I exhaled loudly, not bothering to hide my annoyance. "How many times have I told you my name is Simon? Simon Porte."

"Sorry." Raymond gave a fake little laugh. "I still think of you as Gregory Davenport. My office, please."

As I followed my uncle across the hall, it struck me that he was looking fit, a far cry from the pale, sickly man I'd first met two and a half months ago. But the odor of rotten vegetables of illness still hung about him, something only a person with my super-keen senses would notice.

"Have a seat."

He pointed to a chair, but I remained standing near the doorway. His office gave off negative vibes that kept me on my guard. I didn't much like this relative who had showed up out of the blue at the high school I'd been attending back In Pennsylvania. He had the right credentials, and looked enough like my dad to convince me was my father's older brother. Since I'd just lost my immediate family, I had no choice but to go live with Raymond Davenport and his wife in upstate New York.

Now he sat in his chair behind his power desk and smiled. "I was wondering how you've been. After all, I've been away for the better part of a week."

What is he really after? "I'm the same since you saw me at dinner half an hour ago."

"You're eating well, I noticed. Keeping fit and in great shape."

How weird is this? "Aunt Mary's a good cook."

"But, as I recall, you hardly said a word."

"What should I say?" I asked.

"You might tell me how you like working at Shady Brook Day Camp."

"It's okay."

"Craig – Mr. Averil – says you're doing a great job helping the swim instructor."

I shifted from side to side, eager to leave.

Raymond leaned forward on his desk and winked. "Have a girl friend, do you?"

"Why do you ask?"

"Craig tells me there are some pretty girls at camp."

This is getting ridiculous. "Uncle Raymond, I have to go. My friends are waiting for me."

"You mean Brian Coltrane's twins?"

I didn't much like his snarky tone. "Is there a problem?"

"Of course not. I only wonder if they're your type."

I gave a humorless laugh. "What's my type?"

Andy and Pol were oddballs, all right—chubby Andy, the computer nerd, and his beanpole-skinny sister, Pol, her nose always in a book, music blaring from her ear buds. Sure, they were nothing like the kids I'd hung out with before the accident. Then again, before the accident I'd been a totally different person.

Raymond got to his feet. "I'm going out myself to a town meeting."

I smiled. Interview over. "Have a good one." I turned to leave.

"Be home by ten," Raymond called after me. "You have to get up early in the morning."

"Yeah. Sure." He'd be lucky if I got in by ten-thirty.

I stepped out into the fading daylight and started jogging toward the elementary school five blocks away. I kept to an easy pace the first block or two, upping my speed gradually the way Dad had taught me. I deleted my little chat with Raymond from my thoughts, and began to feel upbeat. Moving fast always improved my mood. Running, swimming, cycling—it didn't matter what I did—as long as my pulse raced and I expended energy. It was the only way I could manage the dark moods that tormented me these days.

I felt a twinge of guilt for mouthing off at my uncle. I was usually respectful to older people, but he bugged me like no one else on this planet. Like calling me Gregory all the time. He knew it bothered the hell out of me, but he kept on doing it. I had no idea why my parents had changed our name from Davenport to Porte, or why I was now Simon when I'd been named Gregory at birth. And now I'd never find out.

I ought to feel grateful to my aunt and uncle for having taken me in, but they were almost as weird as the religious fanatics I'd lived with for two months. Aunt Mary tiptoed around the large house like she was afraid of her own shadow, and Raymond treated me like I was six years old, especially where money was concerned. He doled out ten dollars every Saturday morning like he was handing over a thousand bucks. And he refused to pay the necessary services for my computer and cellphone. I felt totally unconnected without them.

Andy and Pol were waiting for me by the swings. Pol was swaying back and forth, her head bobbing to music she listened to on her iPhone, while her brother fiddled with his.

"You're late," Andy complained, as I knew he would. The kid was a stickler for punctuality.

"Sorry. My uncle just got in from a business trip, and dinner was delayed. Then I had to help my aunt clear the table."

Pol chuckled. "Getting their money's worth out of your hide, are they?"

I sat down on the swing beside her and we moved slowly in tandem. "I don't mind helping around the house. I've had chores to do since I can remember. Besides, Aunt Mary's very...sweet," I finally said. It was kinder than "boring" and "dull."

Andy laughed. "She doesn't say much, does she? Leaves all the talking to Raymond."

"You don't like him," I said.

"Do you?" Pol asked.

I shrugged, not wanting to tell them how much he creeped me out. "I never knew he existed until he brought me here in April. He knows zilch about raising kids."

"He sure knows how to change laws to make himself richer," Andy said.

It amazed me how he and Pol—totally clueless when it came to sports and kids' stuff—knew what was going on around town.

"In fact," Andy went on, "your uncle called the town meeting tonight. Claimed it's something important. I bet we're in for bad news."

I laughed. "And you know this earth-shattering piece of information because?"

"Because knowing what's going on in Buckley is more interesting than memorizing some baseball player's stats. My sources keep my informed."

"Your sources, eh? Well, let me know what you find out about the meeting tonight," I said to change the subject and not because I was interested in my uncle's business affairs.

Andy's eyes blazed with anger. "Raymond Davenport worships the almighty dollar. He builds where he wants and what he wants, and doesn't care if it's good for Buckley. He should be run out of town!"

"Andy, shut up!" Pol said. "You don't bad-mouth someone's relative."

"I'm educating Simon about his Uncle Raymond. If we don't, who will?"

Pol stopped swinging and fixed her gaze on me. It was too dark to see her amazing blue-green eyes, but I felt them studying me.

"Did you hear?" she asked. "A girl died yesterday, over in Chatham Falls."

Death. My stomach started swirling.

"She was going to visit her cousin two blocks away. It was dusk—like it is right now—only she never got there. They found her the next day, lying on the side of a road outside of town."

Andy said, "The weird thing is, there were no wounds or bruises on her body. No sign of strangulation, stabbing, head wound, or gun shot. Just like the other one."

Pol yanked her brother's arm. "We don't need the details."

"You started it. I'm just filling in the facts."

"Poor kid," Pol said. "Melissa went to Shady Brook, but I didn't know her."

A band squeezed my chest so tightly I could barely breathe. "Not Melissa Gordon."

"Uh-huh," Andy said. "They think she was murdered."

"Murdered? I can't believe it. Last week I was teaching her to swim."

"I'm so sorry, Simon," Pol said.

"She was nine years old," I mumbled. "The same age Lucy would be..."

The twins stared at me.

"Who's Lucy?" Pol asked.

I shook my head. "Gotta go."

I took off like a lightning bolt, desperate to get away. I ran down a street I'd never been on before, rubbing away tears brought on by thoughts of my dead sister. I was angry at myself for breaking the one rule I'd set for myself since losing my family: keep your cool, no matter what. But Melissa Gordon! Jeez! She was a cute little thing—two skinny pigtails and a good belly laugh. What monster would kill a kid like that? A few days ago I'd finally got her to put her head in the water. How proud she had been!

I raced across the road and into the path of an SUV. The driver honked, but I was already flying past him.

The twins didn't know Lucy was my baby sister because I'd never told them about the accident that had taken my family and left me an orphan. I knew they wondered why I'd come to live with my aunt and uncle, but for once, even Andy knew not to ask questions.

I gulped down air, forcing myself to run faster. Faster. Still, I couldn't stop the memories from gliding across my brain like a slideshow: camping out with my parents when I was six and Lucy hadn't been born, seeing my first Broadway show, Lucy's second birthday party when…

I finally managed to make my mind go blank. *I have to be strong so I can get through each day.* I said it again and again. I was fifteen years old and alone in the world. The only person I could count on was me.

I slowed down to a jog as I approached Buckley's Main Street. I passed well-lit stores closed for the night, though the supermarket and eating places were still open. People sat at tables outside the coffee house, talking and laughing like they hadn't a care in the world.

I stopped to catch my breath in front of the new glass and brick firehouse half a block away. *Inhale, exhale, inhale, exhale.* I walked in circles until my heart rate returned to normal.

I felt calmer now, more in control. I wouldn't grieve for a little girl I hardly knew. And I wouldn't mull over the past. Brooding served no purpose and got you nowhere.

I retraced my steps to the coffee shop. In the Men's Room, I splashed water on my face then ordered a large soda, which I carried outside. I rarely treated myself from the measly allowance my uncle gave me, but I needed it tonight. I raised the bottle.

CHAPTER ONE

Here's to you, Melissa, I saluted her silently. *May you rest in peace.*

Chapter Two

When I got home, I found Aunt Mary watching TV in the family room. The room was in shadows, and the volume so low, I wondered how she could make out the words.

"Hi, Aunt Mary. I'm back."

She smiled up at me. "Did you have a nice evening with your friends?"

"It was okay."

"There are cookies in the pantry," she said as she did every evening.

"I'm not hungry, thanks. I'm going up to my room."

"Good night then, Simon." She turned back to her program.

Weird! I took the stairs two at a time. Aunt Mary was like a robot. She prepared our meals, kept the house in order, and watched TV at night. She didn't seem to resent having me live with them, but she wasn't welcoming, either. Maybe that was just her personality, since she related to Raymond in the same remote way.

I managed to put aside all thoughts of Melissa and my family, and got ready for bed. I read a few pages of a sci-fi novel Andy had loaned me. When I started yawning. I switched off my lamp and fell asleep. The next thing I knew, my uncle was calling my name.

"Simon, wake up!"

"What's wrong? What happened?" My heart pounded like a jackhammer.

"Time to get up." Raymond turned on my desk lamp.

I looked at the clock. "It's three in the morning! I'm going back to sleep." I pulled the pillow over my head.

"No, you're not!"

He sat on my bed and grabbed my shoulders so I'd face him. "Look at me."

I tried to turn away, but he gripped my chin.

"Cut it out! What's wrong with you? Are you some kind of pervert?"

"Look at me," Raymond repeated. His corneas appeared black, with pinpoints of light where the irises should have been.

I tried to close my eyes, but his gaze held mine as fiercely as his hands clutched my shoulders.

I was falling through space. The pinpoints of light widened into a circle of brightness, and I was in the center. Energy as powerful as electricity poured into my palms. The current gathered momentum and coursed through my body. A pressure expanded inside my head.

"Stop! You're hurting me!"

"Hush," Raymond admonished. "It's almost over. Soon you'll sleep and forget this ever happened."

I moaned. The pressure receded down through my torso, my limbs. *Am I dying? Am I dead?*

A blanket of fatigue stilled my fears and dulled my mind and body. I was barely aware of Raymond settling the covers around me. "Sleep, Gregory, and forget," he whispered as I drifted off.

I awoke the next morning feeling groggy. I let out a yelp as I sat up because my head ached something awful. Bits and pieces of a terrifying nightmare floated to the surface of my mind. The cloaked figure of a man—my uncle?—was hypnotizing me, forcing me to—to—I couldn't remember any more of the dream.

In the bathroom, I swallowed two aspirin dry. I pulled on a bathing suit and a polo shirt, feeling as jumpy as if I'd downed several energy drinks. Come to think of it, I'd had that soda last night. Was it responsible for the strange images passing through my head: an eagle swooping down for its prey; someone getting a blood transfusion in a hospital?

I had to grip the banister for support as I made my way downstairs. I wondered if I was well enough to give swimming lessons today. Even if I wasn't, I was going to camp. No way was I staying in this house another minute longer than I had to.

"Good morning, Simon," Aunt Mary said as I came into the kitchen. "Would you like some orange juice?"

"Yes, please."

I sat at my place at the oval table and drank my juice. I was glad to see that Raymond's place had been cleared.

"Your Uncle Raymond left for the office already. He has a lot of work to catch up on."

Raymond. I frowned as I struggled to remember the awful dream. Raymond was in it. He was trying to—trying to—. Damn! I couldn't bring it back. Maybe the dream had given me the awful headache I woke up with.

"Looks like a nice day today," Aunt Mary commented as she set out cold cereal and milk for my breakfast. Then she sat in her chair and opened the newspaper.

"Anything in the paper about that poor girl who died?" I asked.

"What poor girl are you talking about?"

"Her name's Melissa Gordon. She went to Shady Brook. I used to give her swimming lessons."

"There's no such article in the paper, Simon. Eat your cereal."

"But I am eating." I stopped talking because Aunt Mary had left the kitchen.

I turned on the radio and zipped through stations, hoping to hear something about Melissa. Nothing. I finished my breakfast, then packed my gear bag.

"Aunt Mary, I'm leaving," I shouted up the stairs.

She didn't answer. I shrugged. My aunt and uncle sure were strange. I went outside to wait for the bus. It wouldn't be coming for another ten minutes, but the house was creeping me out.

I leaned against a tree, mulling over my situation. I was beginning to hate it here, as much as I'd hated living with the religious whack-jobs that had me praying on my knees three times a day. Why couldn't I end up with normal people for a change?

Maybe all people turned weird by the time they grew up. Though I'd loved my parents and knew they loved Lucy and me, there was something secretive about them. Like they had something to hide. And that was before I knew they'd changed our name from Davenport to Porte, and I became Simon instead of Gregory.

I waved to a woman who jogged by and a neighbor walking his dog, though I had no idea who they were. Not like my old neighborhood, where I'd known everyone who lived up and down the block.

A skinny, old woman came hobbling up the street. She wore a long purple dress that dragged along the ground. Her messy grey hair tumbled halfway down her back.

I gulped when she stopped inches from me. She was so angry, her blue eyes practically gave off sparks. "Beware of the evil one!"

"Are-are you talking to me?" I asked.

She glared at me. "Of course. Who else? Close your mind to him, my boy! Keep him out! We must thwart him and put a stop to his wickedness, once and for all."

She took off as I found my voice. "What are you talking about?" I called after her, but the old woman continued on her way.

I began to shake. I hugged myself, but it wouldn't stop. *She's just a crazy old lady who escaped the loony bin. Someone's senile grandmother who doesn't know what she's saying.* But her words about the evil one threw me into a funk.

Camp was more hectic than usual because a group of counselors had left to attend Melissa's funeral. A pounding headache, something I never had to deal with before, made it difficult to concentrate on the kids and their water activities. Rick, the waterfront counselor, shouted at me a few times to pay attention to my job. Humiliating, to say the least.

I did my best not to think about my weird dreams or the old woman and her bizarre warning, but I had no control over the vivid scenes that flashed across my mind. They seemed to be memories: of a car trip out West, a prom date with a girl I was crazy about. They *felt* like memories, but I had no idea where they came from because they weren't *my* memories.

The counselors returned to camp at noon, so I was able to eat lunch with Andy and Pol during our one free period of the day. We took our food outside, to one of the wooden tables.

"Are you all right?" Pol asked me.

"I'm fine."

I must have answered rougher than I'd meant to because Andy said, "Hey, bro. She only asked because you're our friend and we care, okay?"

His words moved me. I was too choked up to speak.

Andy must have thought I was still pissed because he said, "We don't want to pry. We know you went through some pretty bad stuff. Else why would you be living with Uncle Raymond?"

I punched his arm. "Thanks."

Pol set her blue-green eyes on me. "Are we good?"

"We're good," I said.

And we were. The tension left my shoulders, and I took a huge bite of my sandwich. As Andy started to talk, another alien memory filled my head, turning his words into background noise.

I was driving at night with a friend, excited because I'd just gotten my license. My friend started telling a joke, and I took my eyes off the road as a truck barreled toward us from the other direction. Terrified, I swerved and drove into some tall bushes. Weird, because I'd never driven a car.

Andy shook my arm. "Earth to Simon."

"Sorry. I was thinking of something."

He thumped his chest. "And I was telling you what happened at the town meeting last night. Remember? You asked me to find out."

"Oh, right."

He pushed his lips from one side to the other, pretending to consider whether or not to continue.

"Your uncle managed to rile up practically everyone in town with his new building plans. He and his cronies will make tons of money building condos, and the town will lose its playing fields."

I forced myself to focus on what Andy was saying. "Back up a bit. What condos? How can he build on land belonging to the town?"

"It's not town land," Pol explained. "It belongs to your family, the Davenports, but was granted to the town for communal use for ninety years. The grant was up two years ago and never renewed."

"Because no one thought it was necessary!" Andy shouted. The kids at the next table stared at him. Andy lowered his voice. "It was a given. Kids play soccer and baseball there most of the year."

"I can't see why you're getting all worked up. You don't play soccer or baseball," Pol said.

Andy looked shocked. "It's the principle of the thing! Raymond Davenport's a bloodsucking tyrant. He'll take away those kids' playing fields just to make a couple of million dollars, which he doesn't need, for sure!"

Pol glared at her twin. "That's Simon's uncle you're talking about."

Andy gave me a sheepish smile. "My apologies, Simon."

I waved my hand. "Forget it. Can't the townspeople do anything?"

"A lawyer's looking into it," Pol said. "Dad says they'll hold a town meeting to discuss it, but not till September, when everyone's back from vacation."

"By then it will be too late," Andy said mournfully.

Raymond planned to take away the kids' playing fields. Something else to hold against my uncle.

I headed for the pool area to watch over the next period's group of swimmers. I felt better. My headache was gone, and so were the strange scenes that felt like memories. It was as though someone had hosed down my mind, clearing it of cobwebs and weird thoughts. My senses were keen and alert.

I greeted the group of eight-year-old boys and took charge of the four Rick wanted me to work with. I told them to grab paddle boards and to kick to the far end of the pool. When they got there, one little boy whispered something in his neighbor's ear.

"Timmy," I called to him, "if you have an earache, you shouldn't be in the pool."

Timmy stared up at me, furious at being found out. "Ah, gee, Simon. How could you hear—?"

"Out!" I ordered. "What did you do with the note your mother sent in?"

"It's in my locker." Tim splashed as he left the pool. "I'll give it to the nurse."

"Make sure you do that."

"All right. Now kick back across the pool then we'll work on your strokes," I told the others.

The three boys stared at me goggle-eyed, like I was Spiderman. For the rest of the period they obeyed every instruction I issued without one complaint.

What's happening to me? I did my best to suppress the panic rising in my chest.

I'd been three years old when my extra-keen senses kicked in.

Suddenly I could hear what people down the block were saying. I knew their thoughts, what they were feeling, and it nearly drove me bonkers. I ran around with my hands on my ears, screaming and crying.

My dad realized something was wrong. When I explained what I was going through as best I could, he taught me how to close myself to extraneous stimuli through concentration and a form of self-hypnosis. It took time, but I mastered the technique until I did it automatically.

Only today the technique wasn't working. My hearing was sharper than ever, and the kids' emotions resounded in my skull like heavy metal music. When the boys went inside to change out of their wet suits, I found a quiet corner in the cafeteria and consciously went through what Dad had taught me all those years ago. I felt calmer. I met the next group of swimmers, and was relieved to discover I'd blocked out their thoughts and feelings, and could concentrate on their lesson.

But why was I suddenly vulnerable after all these years?

When the bus dropped me off, the old woman was waiting. This time she didn't frighten me, probably because she no longer looked angry.

"Don't let him win," she said softly, fixing her blue eyes on mine.

"You mean my uncle?"

"Protect yourself from evil."

"I will," I promised, though I had no idea what she was talking about. She took off down the block, moving pretty fast for an old lady.

Suddenly I had lots of questions. "Who are you?" I shouted after her. "How do you know what you know?"

She turned. "Because I do." She continued on her way.

Chapter Three

Aunt Mary was in her usual place in the dimly-lit family room watching television at a barely audible volume.

"Hey, Aunt Mary, how are you?"

"Fine, dear." Her voice sounded thick, as if she'd been crying. "Dinner's at six. Your uncle promised to be home by then."

"Okay."

She turned back to her program. I stood there, picking up on what she felt—an overwhelming sadness mingled with pity.

The pity is for me.

Why pity? Because my family was dead? No, it had to do with something recent. Something that kept her from looking me in the eye.

I suddenly remembered Andy's telling me about my uncle's many business deals. The man was loaded. He could easily afford to hook up my computer and smartphone.

A wave of anger swept over me. I diffused it and changed it to iron resolve. I felt strong. Invincible! *They'll give me what I need or else!*

"Aunt Mary."

"Yes, dear?"

"I need money."

"Doesn't your uncle give you an allowance every week?" she asked.

I gave a snort. "I'm fifteen years old. I need more than the measly

16

ten dollars he doles out like it's gold."

"I'm sure your uncle knows what he's doing."

"He knows zip about teenagers. Probably because he has no kids of his own."

"Simon!" Aunt Mary gasped, but there was no stopping me.

"This is the twenty-first century, Aunt Mary. The Age of Electronics, in case you haven't noticed."

How had I lived all these months without my laptop and smartphone? Letting my uncle keep me on a string of ten dollars a week? Sending me to camp with sandwiches?

I felt like a bear awakening from his winter hibernation. I felt like roaring.

"Either he comes across or I'm taking off."

That caught her attention. She stared at me, her mouth wide open. "Don't say that, Simon. I'll speak to your uncle."

"You'd better," I muttered, taking the stairs two at a time.

Wow! Where did that come from? I stretched out on my bed, suddenly too exhausted to wonder about the strange mood swings and thoughts affecting me all day. Minutes later I was sound asleep.

Aunt Mary woke me for dinner. "You slept so soundly, I was beginning to worry," she said.

"I must have been really tired," I said, hoping that was the reason for my peculiar thoughts and behavior earlier in the day. I felt like me once again as I followed Aunt Mary downstairs.

Raymond was in high spirits as he brought in the steaks he'd barbecued on the grill. After Aunt Mary served the salad and baked potatoes, he announced he'd made some advantageous contacts regarding his new condo building venture.

Aunt Mary cleared her throat. "You're going ahead with your plans to build on the playing fields?

"Of course. The land belongs to the Davenports, and I'm a Davenport, my dear." He stuck a forkful of meat into his mouth and chewed noisily.

Aunt Mary stared at him. "Don't you think you should wait until the town meeting in September?"

"Why? Most of the townspeople want to leave the property as is, but that's too bad. The grant ended years ago. I can do what I like."

"What if *she* interferes?" Aunt Mary asked.

Who is she? I wondered.

Raymond laughed. "*She's* too gaga to do anything." He reached across to pat Aunt Mary's hand. "It will mean more money for us, and nice new homes for some people in town."

Aunt Mary let out a deep sigh as if she were resigned to Raymond's plans. He talked enthusiastically about the project. Aunt Mary got caught up in his excitement and began asking questions about the condo plans.

My uncle winked at me. "I bet you're surprised your Aunt Mary knows so much about construction."

I shrugged.

"She used to work with me. Ran the office when I was out of town."

"Why did you stop working?" I asked.

Neither of them answered. Raymond's smile disappeared. Older people's secrets, I thought.

"We hoped to have a family," Aunt Mary said. "Only things didn't work out that way."

"Until now!" Raymond boomed, reaching over to pat my shoulder. I flinched when he touched a sore spot that had been bothering me all day. The smell of rotting vegetables, though barely noticeable now, made me queasy. How had he recovered almost completely from the illness that had plagued him back in April?

Since he was in such a good mood, now was the time to hit him with my request.

"Uncle Raymond, I need a decent allowance. Ten dollars a week doesn't cut it no how."

His eyebrows shot up. "Is that so?" he asked in mock surprise.

I opened my mouth to argue, and closed it again. Arguing would get me nowhere. Raymond frowned, betraying his disappointment that I hadn't exploded in anger, which he would have slapped down as insubordination.

He's testing you, an inner voice explained. *Challenging you, yet hoping you'll win. Then he wins, too.*

What was that all about?

I drew a deep breath and spoke in a calm and reasonable tone. "I need money for lots of things. My computer's still not hooked up. You never did get me a high speed provider as you said you would."

"I've been busy, son. Besides, it costs."

"Not that much since you already have a computer in the house."

"Which is available for you to use."

I grimaced. "Sure, as long as you're in the house and not using it yourself, which isn't very often. I've had my own computer since I was six years old."

Raymond's face flushed with anger. "Maybe that's how your parents raised you. In this house we do things differently."

My parents. I had a flash of insight. "What did you do with my money?"

Raymond bristled. "What money are you talking about?"

"The money I inherited from my parents. The money from the sale of my family's house?"

"Where do you think it is? Some is in a savings account, the rest is in safe investments. You'll have it all when you turn twenty-one."

I glared at him, and enjoyed the satisfaction of watching him jerk back in his chair. "I'd like some of it now so I can upgrade my computer and buy myself a camera. And I'll need a credit card so I don't have to ask for money every time I want to go to the movies."

"You never go to the movies!"

"Maybe I would if I didn't have to beg for a handout," I answered calmly. I had no idea why I was suddenly in control of the situation or what I was about to say next. Only that it would continue until I got what I wanted.

"Damn it, Simon. This is my house!"

"Yes, but a judge may see things my way."

"What judge? What the hell are you talking about?"

"I'll petition the family court and tell the judge you're stingy with my money, and I'm unhappy living here."

Raymond's eyes almost popped out of his head. I had to press my lips together to keep from grinning. He was furious, and behind the fury ran a streak of fear. Fear of what? I had no idea.

"I'll hand over five hundred dollars of your own damn money, which you can do with as you like! And show you the monthly bank statements to prove I'm not cheating you of one red cent!"

"I wasn't doubting your honesty, Uncle Raymond, but from now on I'll look over the statements every month. It's time I learned about finances."

He glared at me. Slowly, his frown turned into a broad smile. He leaned across the table to pat me on the shoulder.

"You're going to make a good businessman, Simon. Just like your uncle." Discussion closed. He was thoroughly pleased with himself as he concentrated on his food.

I forced myself to do the same. Something was wrong. I'd won the battle. So why was Raymond happy? And it was weird how I now knew which buttons to push when arguing with him. Almost as though I was beginning to think like him.

A ridiculous thought, but it managed to send chills down my back.

* * *

I helped clear the table, and raced out of the house. I ran the eight blocks to Andy and Pol's house nonstop.

Mrs. Coltrane greeted me with a smile. "Hi, Simon. Andy's on his computer, as usual. Pol's downloading music on her phone."

"Thanks, Mrs. C."

"There are fudge cookies and peach ice cream if you kids get hungry," Mrs. Coltrane said, returning to her husband and the TV in the den.

"Great!"

I bounded up the steep flight of stairs, and headed for Andy's bedroom. The house was smaller and less elegant than my aunt and uncle's, but it hummed with life and activity.

"Hey," I greeted Andy, and collapsed on his rumpled bedspread.

"Be with you in a minute. I'm downloading this program for one of the kids. Almost done."

"Take your time," I said, and meant it. Being here reminded me of my own home.

Pol wandered into the room. "I thought I heard you coming up the stairs."

Andy spun around on his chair. "Yeah, like a herd of elephants."

I reached behind me for Andy's pillow and tossed it at him. Andy grabbed one of his slippers and threw it at me. It hit a lamp shade.

"Cut it out!" Pol complained. "You're acting like a bunch of baboons."

"You want to play this great game?" Andy asked me. "I downloaded it last night."

"All right."

The game was pretty awesome, and soon I was too engrossed in it to think of anything else. Knights in a small kingdom battled each other to become leader. Then they united to fight against knights from other small kingdoms. Then they realigned, according to their wins, to fight for control of the central government of the entire country. Each level introduced new weapons the knights could fight with, weapons that

21

required learning and skill.

Andy won the first round, but I beat him in the next two.

"Break time!" Pol declared, entering the room with a tray of cookies, ice cream, and soda.

"Can you play this game alone?" I asked.

"Sure, but it's not as much fun. Why do you ask? Your computer's not connected."

"It will be soon," I said, grinning. "I've convinced my uncle I need my electronic devices."

"How did you manage that?" Pol asked. "Raymond Davenport usually calls the shots."

I shrugged, not wanting to talk about my uncle. There were too many things about him I needed to figure out first.

Instead, I said, "This morning, a funny old lady spooked me while I was waiting for the bus. She shouted out some really strange things, and did it again when I got home from camp."

"What did she look like?" Pol asked.

"She had long, straggly gray hair and wore a dress down to the ground."

"What did she say?" Andy demanded.

I pretended I couldn't remember, though her words were branded in my memory. "Some kind of warning. About evil."

Pol laughed. "That sounds like Lucinda Davenport."

I gaped at her. "Davenport? You mean she's a relative of mine?"

"She's your Uncle Raymond's aunt," Andy said.

"Your grandfather's sister," Pol explained. "Lucinda was always strange. Mom says she grows weirder the older she gets."

I swallowed, dreading to ask the next question. "Did you know my grandparents?"

"We used to see them around town," Pol said. "After your grandmother died, your grandfather moved to Florida. Did you ever visit him there?"

"Never!" I felt a flush of red anger at my parents. Andy and Pol had known my grandparents, and I'd never had the chance to meet them.

"Weird!" Andy commented. "Though I wouldn't mind if Mom and Dad cut the cord to most of our aunts and uncles."

It suddenly struck me. "Her name's Lucinda!"

"Yep," Andy said.

I took a deep breath, terrified because I was about to break my privacy rule. "I wonder if Lucy was named after her."

"Who's Lucy?" Pol asked, as she had the night before.

"My sister."

The twins exchanged surprised glances. I could see they wanted to ask me a million questions, but their good manners held them in check.

"She died with my parents in an auto accident. She would have turned nine in May."

"Sorry, dude." Andy gave my arm a half-hearted punch.

Pol simply nodded. She turned quickly away, hoping I hadn't seen her tears.

I stared ahead, at the blank wall. "It happened during Winter Vacation. I'd been on a skiing trip in Vermont with a group from school—working ferociously on my christies during the day, smooching with Ariana Cutherson till all hours of the night. I was having the time of my life, and barely gave a thought to my family.

"Lucy texted me the last evening of the trip. She was frightened because our parents were acting weird. I calmed her down, and reminded her they usually acted weird. I got her to laugh, and said I'd see her when I got home. A few minutes later my father called to say they were coming to pick me up, and should be arriving some time after midnight.

"'Why are you coming all the way to Vermont?' I asked.

"'Just do as you're told,' Dad said. He apologized for snapping and said he and my mom loved me very much."

"That is a little—" Andy said.

"Bizarre. I know." I swiped at the tears on my face. Pol handed me a tissue, and I blew my nose. "I've gone over it again and again, and I still can't figure out why they drove up to Vermont that night.

"It began to snow. Dad wasn't a great driver under ordinary circumstances. It was stupid, their coming all the way to Vermont when I was going home on the bus the following day. I called my parents to tell them this, but both their cell phones were out of service.

"Midnight came and went. I started to panic. Was the drive taking longer because of the weather, or were they stuck in a snowdrift? One of the teachers stayed with me in the motel lobby while I paced up and down the carpet. He finally fell asleep, and so did I. A policeman woke me up at dawn. There'd been an accident, he told me. The car exploded. My parents and Lucy were killed."

"How awful," Andy said. "Did a car crash into them?"

"There was no other car. The police said the cause was inconclusive, whatever that means."

We sat in silence. I tried desperately to remember what I'd known about my parents' lives. They had no close friends. They never involved themselves in community activities, and remained on cordial but distant terms with our neighbors. It was almost as though they were hiding from something. Or someone.

But Mom had been close to her sister. Aunt Grace was to be Lucy and my guardian if anything ever happened to our parents. She must have been out of the country at the time of the accident, since the authorities couldn't contact her. But surely she was back home by now! Why didn't I think of this before? I'd call her the minute I had my cellphone back in service.

But first I had another relative to contact. "Where does my Great-

Aunt Lucinda live?"

Pol fixed her all-knowing eyes on me. "On Willow Road, two blocks past the high school. You're going to visit her?"

My heart pounded against my ribcage. "Maybe."

"Be careful," Andy warned. "People say she's a witch."

"You're kidding. Right?"

Pol shrugged. "You saw how she looks and acts. Stories get started, probably as jokes. Though some people swear strange things have happened."

"Sometimes they do," Andy said. "Come on, Pol. You heard that when a Canadian guy tried to rob Lucinda's house, a demon flew out and broke his arm."

Pol rolled her eyes. "Like I said — stories. Turns out, Lucinda was home and took care of the robber by herself with a rolling pin."

I stood. "I'll see you guys tomorrow."

Pol shot me her inscrutable smile. "It's the only stone house on Willow."

Chapter Four

L ucinda's house was set far back from the road, behind an overgrown tangle of trees and shrubs. Kind of like the woods Hansel and Gretel got lost in. Lucy used to beg to hear that story again and again, even after she could read it herself. She'd liked it because it showed kids were so smart, they could outwit a witch.

A witch! I stared at my great-aunt's front door, and told myself Lucinda wasn't a witch. There was no such creature, at least not in the fairy tale way! I pulled back my shoulders and, not seeing a bell, knocked.

She opened it a minute later, her bright blue eyes raking me up and down like cat's claws. "Clever boy, you found your way."

My heart leaped into my mouth, and I turned to run. My aunt's cackle chased after me.

"Don't be afraid. I'm your Great-Aunt Lucinda, and I've things to tell you. Come along, Gregory." She spun around and walked through the cozy sitting room, not waiting to see if I was following.

"My name's Simon," I said when we stopped in the kitchen at the back of the house. "Don't call me Gregory."

"That's what they named you when you were born," Lucinda said. She pointed to the table against the kitchen wall, and I sat down. "I should know. I saw you when you were five minutes old."

"You did?"

I stared at Lucinda, but she was pulling a dish from the oven. I became aware of the delicious aroma wafting through the small house.

"Apple crumb cake," she announced, setting it on top of the stove. "I hope you have room for a piece or two, after everything you scoffed down at your friends' house."

"Well, sure. I'd love a piece, but how did you know...?"

"I know lots of things, Gregory, most of which I wish I could erase from my mind for the pain they cause."

"Please don't call me Gregory. He calls me that."

"Your Uncle Raymond." Lucinda grimaced. "He's some piece of work, isn't he?"

"He took me in. I'm grateful for that."

"He did it for his sake, not yours." She let loose a cackle of laughter. "Raymond only does what serves Raymond. He's evil through and through."

Her words sent a shiver down my back.

She cut me a square of apple cake. "Bite in. Tell me how it tastes."

It had to be the best apple cake ever. "It's awesome!"

Lucinda grinned, showing teeth yellowed with age. She had to be at least eighty-five years old. "Your father always liked my apple cake."

My heart began to race. "You knew my father?"

"Of course. Edward was my nephew, wasn't he? Same as Raymond. Only those two boys had nothing in common. I'll pour you a glass of milk."

Lucinda set the glass in front of me and added hot water to her mug of tea. I sipped and ate, wondering which of the many questions swarming around in my head to ask first. Before I could decide, Lucinda got in a question of her own.

"You thought I was a nutter, didn't you, saying those things to you out in broad daylight?"

I nodded.

She grinned, clearly pleased with herself. "It was the only way to grab your attention. As it is, the people of Buckley think I'm mad. I tell them what I know to be true, and they laugh at me."

I thought back to what she'd said to me earlier in the day. "Uncle Raymond's evil?"

Lucinda nodded. "Indeed, he is. It's not all his fault, but he's made the most of our curse. He's the worst of the lot."

I blinked, confused. "I don't understand. What's he done?"

"Terrible things, judging by his sudden good health."

"Yeah, I noticed he looks much better than he did when I first met him. But what terrible things are you talking about?"

Lucinda seemed to shrink within herself as her cheeriness disappeared. I noticed the sunken cheeks, the wrinkles on her face. She reminded me of an old gnarled tree.

"Our family isn't like other families, but I'm sure you know that by now."

'I really don't. I never met any of my father's relatives until after the accident."

"That's because your father tried to protect you. But he didn't do a good job of it, because here you are again, back in Buckley and living with Raymond."

Frustrated, I pounded the table. "I still don't know what you're talking about! Would you please tell me what you mean?"

"Your father never told you anything about his family? Never explained why he and your mother grabbed you and sped away in the dead of night?"

I shook my head.

"Your father was an honorable man. He considered the powers some members of our family have to be evil. And he was right."

"That word again – evil. It so old-fashioned."

"It's evil to drain young people of their lives so you can live longer."

The awful image of a plastic tube being thrust down a little girl's throat flashed in my mind. "Melissa Gordon," I murmured.

Lucinda nodded, her expression grim. "And there were others. Why do you think Raymond's brimming with good health these days?"

I stared at her, wishing I'd never come to this house. This town. "If you know, why don't you tell the police! Do something, so there won't be any more murders!"

Lucinda pounded the table with her fist. "Don't you think I've tried? But I've no proof, just my own hideous knowledge." Her voice lowered to a mumble. "Besides, I've my own checkered past to live down."

I suddenly envisioned a bikini-clad young Lucinda riding a white horse through town. Now where did that come from?

"The people of Buckley see Raymond as a wealthy entrepreneur and respected member of the town council, while I've been labeled a witch. If I insist Raymond's behind all those children's deaths, he'll find a way to lock me up in a psychiatric ward."

What kind of family do I come from? No wonder my parents ran from this town. "Are you a witch?" I asked.

"Of course not! And I'm not like Raymond, his father and my grandfather—all capable of draining another person's life force to enhance theirown. But my senses are heightened, well beyond the ordinary range. Last night they fairly shook me like my own personal hurricane. I figured it had something to do with Raymond." She gazed at me, her expression gentle. "And you."

"Me?" I shuddered. "But he hasn't done anything to me. I mean, I don't especially like him, but…"

"As I said, everything Raymond does has a reason, a reason that serves Raymond Davenport. He's evil, Gregory — I mean, Simon. You must close yourself to him."

"Close myself." I echoed the familiar expression. "My dad taught me to do that when I was little. Bizarre thoughts and images used to fill my head and drive me nuts. I learned how to block them, and eventually it became automatic. Until today."

"You've learned to close yourself automatically, but there are other methods of attack." Lucinda squinted at me. "Are you absolutely positive Raymond didn't hypnotize you?"

I thought a bit. "I had this weird dream in the middle of the night. I woke up with a headache and what seemed like memories, only they weren't *my* memories. Do you think Raymond did that?"

My great-aunt stared at me with terror in her eyes. "My God! That's something no Davenport has dared to try since Uncle Frank's fiasco."

"You're scaring me. What are you talking about?"

"You should be scared, Simon. Raymond hypnotized you and performed an infusion. He intends to take over your mind and body."

I shivered as an arctic cold blasted through me. "Then where will I be?"

Lucinda closed her eyes. "As good as buried thirty feet beneath the ground."

Chapter Five

My first impulse was to run, run as far as I could—out of Buckley, New York, maybe the country. Lucinda must have sensed my panic, because she led me into the living room and sat me down on the sofa. Her bony hand on mine was surprisingly comforting.

"Think, boy, before you take off half-crazed. I have about forty dollars to give you, and where would that take you? Your uncle's no fool. He'll have a manhunt after you before you leave the county."

She was right. My heart fluttered like a bird trapped in an attic. "I won't go back to that house! He'll do that infusion thing again!" I put my hands over my head. "I don't want his thoughts and memories inside me!"

"This time you'll be ready for him."

I stared at Lucinda. She was my great-aunt and she meant well, but she was a bit loony herself. "I'm no match for Uncle Raymond."

"You've powers of your own, Simon. I sensed them this morning." She
grinned. "For one thing, I bet your hearing's especially acute."
"It is."

Lucinda's expression hardened. "My baby brother had a sharp ear. It's part of a special combination of talents. Too bad he was done away with at age nine."

"Done away with?" My heart, which was racing, began to beat even faster. "You mean somebody killed him?"

"His own grandfather. For the life force." She snorted. "Don't worry, I paid him back as soon as I could. Sent his blood spurting like a geyser."

I stared at her, horrified to learn that she, too, had murdered. "What did they do to you?"

"Nothing." Lucinda shrugged. "There wasn't a mark on him, so the police had nothing to go on. But my parents knew. They didn't want to lose another child, so they sent me to live with cousins in Canada."

"No wonder my parents left Buckley."

"Of course." Lucinda's tone softened. "Edward had no stomach for the family's talents and vices. He wanted to live a normal life."

I buried my face in my hands. "Do you think Raymond killed my parents?"

Lucinda shook her head. "I couldn't say, but I wouldn't put it past him if he wanted you."

The thought that my uncle might have killed my parents ignited a flame of resolve that burned away some of my terror. "I'll make him pay somehow."

"You can only make him pay by defeating him, completely and thoroughly."

"You mean actually kill him? I don't know if I can do that."

"Let's take first things first. You said your father taught you to close your mind."

"Yes."

"Good. That's a start. Show me how you do it."

I closed my eyes and stilled my thoughts as Dad had taught me to do when I was three years old. The cloud of peace that usually took the color of lavender filled my mind, ridding it of all outside influences. An alien force tried to

intrude, but I blocked it.

32

"Very good," Lucinda said after a while. "You were able to resist my will."

Still in a dreamy state, I smiled. "Today in camp I was able to zoom in on some of the younger kids' emotions. That never happened before."

Lucinda cackled with glee. "Raymond would have a fit if he knew his infusions were enhancing your powers. Now I'll show you a trick or two how to resist the effect of his infusions."

We spent the next half hour working on my powers of concentration. At last Lucinda was satisfied. "That should staunch most of his evil."

"Most of it?" I didn't like the sound of this.

Lucinda frowned. "Raymond has more experience at this than you do, but on a deeper level you're more than his match. The trick is to let him think he's taking over your mind without letting him go far."

My heart nearly jumped into my throat. "But what if he pushes past my barriers? What if he takes over and I can't stop him?"

Lucinda's eyes flashed like two lasers. "I promise you, that will not happen. Raymond's attempting something new, something he's never tried before. He's basically a cautious man. He'll go slow and gradual. You've enough power and control to ward him off for the time being. When you need to heighten your powers, we'll work together."

"Shall I come here?" I asked.

"No. By then Raymond will suspect I'm helping you, and have lookouts watching both of us."

"Lookouts! As in spies?"

"Of course. My nephew Raymond was always one to delegate work. Beware of anyone who tries to get close to you."

She closed her eyes. After a minute, she said, "Four, eight, six, one. Remember those numbers. When you want to contact me, repeat those numbers over and over again in your head. I'll get in touch with you as soon as I can."

"Four, eight, six, one," I repeated. I felt light-headed as I stood. "All this stuff you've told me—it's like a sci-fi movie. I can hardly take it all in."

"It is a lot to absorb," Lucinda agreed. "More than you should have to at one clip. But you have no choice." She circled her hands in front of my face.

"I'm invoking a spell of composure. It will help calm you down yet keep your head clear. Now leave before your aunt and uncle start worrying about your whereabouts and he goes out searching for you."

To my surprise, Lucinda grabbed me around the waist and hugged me tight. I hugged her back, overwhelmed by a wave of affection for my new-found relative. It dawned on me that she was the first person I'd hugged since losing my family.

"Thanks, Aunt Lucinda. I'm glad to know you're in the picture."

She patted my cheek. "You're a good boy, Simon. I'm terribly sorry about your father and mother. They were good people."

* * *

It was close to eleven o'clock when I crept into the house. I stepped warily into the darkened hall, hoping not to meet my uncle. I'd made it halfway up the stairs, when he called to me from below.

"You're coming in later and later, I see."

I looked down. Uncle Raymond stood in the hall outside his office. *Monster!* I prayed he hadn't been waiting for me to come home so he could give me another infusion.

"I lost track of the time," I said, hating the way my voice shook.

Raymond didn't answer. I began to tremble. I knew what he was capable of. Despite Lucinda's pep talk, I couldn't stop him from doing what he liked.

Calm down. I have to calm down. I drew a few deep breaths. Raymond still hadn't moved. "I'm going up to bed," I said, meeting his gaze head on. Though he stood in the shadows, I managed to read his expression. He was anxious rather than angry. "I don't like your staying out so late. Don't forget, you have to get up early for camp."

"Don't worry. I can handle it."

I felt a prodding sensation. Raymond was trying to read my mind. I blocked him, and nearly laughed at the startled expression that crossed his face.

Then Raymond smiled, but it looked like he was in pain. "I'm only concerned about your health, Simon."

Sure you are. I dashed up to the rest of the stairs. When I got to the landing, I called down. "Uncle Raymond."

"Yes?"

"Please don't forget to put the money in my account, and to set up an internet provider so I can use my computer."

"I'll take care of it first thing in the morning."

I closed my bedroom door and jammed the desk chair under the handle so I wouldn't be caught unawares if Raymond tried another of his infusions. I undressed and slipped into bed.

I turned off the lamp and realized I could see everything in the room, plain as day. I blinked a few times. Nothing changed. I saw my desk, the bureau, my jeans on the chair where I'd left them.

I shut my eyes and drifted off to sleep, aware of this last surprise in a day full of surprises. I could see in the dark.

Chapter Six

I awoke the next morning, surprised that I'd managed to sleep the whole night through. I felt rested and relaxed until my feet hit the floor, and my mind started churning like clothes in a dryer. What kind of family did I come from? I was living in a house with a ghoul. My own uncle—my father's older brother—wanted to take over my body and my mind because his were wearing out!

Panic rose inside me, and it took all my efforts to calm myself down. It didn't make sense to run away or to show Raymond I was on to him. My only chance was to outsmart him. How? I didn't know yet, but there had to be a way out of this horror house.

I got dressed and came downstairs, relieved that Raymond didn't make an appearance at the breakfast table. At camp, I had a busy morning giving swimming lessons to three groups in a row. When lunch time came, I slipped onto the bench across from Andy and Pol.

"Pay your Aunt Lucinda a visit last night?" Andy asked, chomping on his sandwich.

"Uh-huh." I wanted to tell them what we talked about, but how could I? They'd think I was crazy. High on drugs. They'd be horrified to know that my uncle Raymond was responsible for little Melissa's death.

"Was she glad to see you?" Pol asked.

"Aunt Lucinda? I think so."

"You think so!" Andy echoed derisively. "Don't you know?"

"Yeah, she was glad to see me," I said flatly.

"What did you talk about?"

I stared at her. It was a typical Pol question, but she seemed awfully curious. Was she pumping me for information? Lucinda said not to trust anyone. Was my uncle using Andy and Pol as spies? Keeping tabs on what I was thinking and planning to do?

Nah, it was a crazy idea, but I was in a crazy situation and couldn't take chances.

"We talked about our family," I finally said. "I got the impression Great-Aunt Lucinda doesn't much like Uncle Raymond."

"I can't imagine why," Andy said. "He's such a snake. I bet he's planning to go ahead with the condos deal, regardless of what the town wants."

"I don't know what he's planning," I said.

Pol cut me a sharp look like she didn't believe me. I felt my ears heating up. I didn't know why I'd lied. It wasn't like I cared about the condo deal, one way or the other, while it meant a lot to Andy. I was following my instincts to lay low and not say anything important to anyone, including the only two friends I had in Buckley.

I bit into my sandwich. The twins said nothing. I wanted to break the tension, but I had no information I wanted to share.

"Well, see you tonight at the playground," Andy said as he went to toss his garbage in the pail.

"Right, see you at eight."

I watched them walk off, relieved that they weren't angry with me enough to stop our evening ritual.

Too soon it was time to go home. I felt nervous as the bus brought me closer and closer to my aunt and uncle's home. How could I possibly act normal around Raymond, knowing the creep planned to take over my body? My hands closed into fists as I thought about my family. I owed it to my parents and Lucy to find out if Raymond had murdered them.

But how? I sure could use Pol and Andy's help, but was afraid to bring them in. Much as they disliked Raymond, they'd have a hard time believing just how evil he was. For another, Lucinda had warned me not to trust anyone. For the entire ride, I circled around the problem, wishing I could find a way in.

I exited the bus as my uncle was saying good-bye to a technician in a white van. Raymond threw an arm around my shoulders, and I had no choice but to walk like we were pals into the house.

"I got your computer all hooked up like you asked me to. Come see for yourself."

I flew up the stairs two at a time. Raymond laughed as he followed at a slower pace.

I logged onto my email and started reading the hundreds of posts waiting for me. Most of the personal ones were months old, expressing sympathy. The rest were from sites I subscribed to. I scrolled down, skimming and deleting.

"Is the provider fast enough for you?" Raymond asked.

I turned, surprised to find him still in my room. I forced a smile. "Sure is. Thanks, Uncle Raymond."

He placed a checkbook and some bills next to the monitor. "And I've opened an account for you. There's four hundred and seventy-five dollars in it and some checks to get you started. You'll have to stop by the bank to arrange for a pin number for the ATM machine. Here's forty dollars in cash."

I opened the checkbook, relieved that the account was made out to Simon Porte.

"Thanks, Uncle Raymond. What about my smart phone?"

"Remind me a day or two, and you'll have that up and running, too."

"Great." I turned back to the monitor and the mountain of emails.

"Well, I'll leave you to it then," he said as he left my room.

It seemed only fifteen minutes had passed when Aunt Mary called to come downstairs to set the table.

"Coming," I shouted back. I washed my hands and started down the steps. I wondered why I felt different. Not different, I realized, just without the weight of the world pressing down on my shoulders. It was how I used to be before the accident. For two solid hours I'd blocked out the horror that had become my life.

Don't forget for one minute what Raymond has planned. I had to be vigilant. I couldn't let down my guard.

After dinner, I returned to my room to continue sorting through my emails. I'd contacted a few of my friends, and they'd written back. I needed to find out what was happening in my old neighborhood. My parents had no close friends there, but I did. Maybe I could find a way to live there.

I paid no attention to the ringing of the phone until Aunt Mary knocked on my half-closed door. "It's Andy Coltrane."

I took the phone from her.

"Hey, Simon, did you forget about us? Pol and I are waiting for you in the playground."

I looked at the clock. "Jeez, it's twenty past eight! Sorry."

Andy grunted. "Well, that's just great. We've been waiting for you for almost half an hour and you're sorry. What gives?"

I realized I'd hurt his feelings and I had to make amends.

"I lost track of the time," I said as I walked back to my room. "I finally got my computer hooked up, and I've been catching up with people I haven't heard from in months."

"You can get on line any time. Come on down to the playground ASAP. Pol and I want to talk to you about something important."

A message from my friend, Paul, whom I'd just contacted, appeared on the screen. "Can it hold till tomorrow? I'm in the middle of something, and I don't want to lose my trend of thought."

Andy expelled an exaggerated sigh of exasperation. "I suppose. It would have been nice if you'd bothered to tell us you weren't coming in the first place."

"I said I was sorry. Talk to you tomorrow."

I replaced the phone on my uncle's night table then hurried back to my computer. I answered my friend's email, deleted a bunch of advertisements, then scrolled up to the beginning of the list to make sure I hadn't missed anything important. I spotted one with an unfamiliar email address. The subject line read "Gretel."

I was about to delete it, when I remembered how much Lucy loved "Hansel and Gretel."

The message was in an attachment: "Simon, show this to no one! Call the number then erase the message ASAP." It was followed by a telephone number. I didn't recognize the area code.

My fingers shook as I jotted down the number on a slip of paper, which I tucked in my shorts' pocket. I was nervous and excited. For sure this was from someone who knew that my parents and Lucy had been murdered. Why else would someone instruct me to delete the message and keep it secret if he didn't know about evil Raymond?

I headed back to the phone in my aunt and uncle's room, then decided it wasn't safe to call from the house. My uncle was out, but might return at any minute. Besides, he could trace the number of any call made on the house phone. I'd waited all these months; I'd play it safe and make the call when I had my cell phone back in service.

I stayed at the computer until my aunt called up the stairs to say it was ten-thirty and maybe I should be thinking about getting ready for bed.

"Thanks, Aunt Mary. Fifteen minutes more and I'm hopping into the shower."

But an hour later I was still at the computer, engrossed in reading movie reviews. Now that I had spending money, I intended to catch up on all the movies I'd missed these past few months. I heard someone enter the room, but was intent on finishing the page on the screen. I gave a start when I realized Raymond had come to stand beside my chair.

"I see you're happy to have your computer up and running again, but it's well past midnight."

"I'm turning it off in a minute."

"Simon."

I glanced up and met my uncle's gaze. In the dim light, Raymond's grey eyes turned black. They glowed like coals. I tried to look away, tried to shut my eyes, but couldn't do anything but stare back.

"Gregory," he murmured.

I opened my mouth to say that wasn't my name, but no words came from my throat. Raymond's eyes glowed red then yellow, as they drew me into a vortex. I felt like I was on a carnival ride that kept me off-center.

"No!" I silently shouted. I had to close myself off, but how could I when something had already entered my mind, changing my memories, my thoughts?

He's got me! Knowing what my uncle intended, what I was enduring at the moment, threw me into a panic. I thought of Great-Aunt Lucinda and quivered as my uncle roared with laughter.

"Don't fight it. Nothing and no one can help you, my boy. Soon you'll be me. Or rather, I'll be you." That awful laughter again. "I've no idea where *you'll* be, Simon or Gregory."

I gripped the arms of my chair and forced myself to calm down, to concentrate. No easy task, with the images and memories churning about in my head. I gritted my teeth at the sight of a young girl gasping her last breath. *Focus. I must focus.*

I drew a deep breath and exhaled slowly as Lucinda had taught me.

My heartbeat slowed. My uncle's mind pressed against mine, and my defenses rose to the challenge. Surprised, Raymond backed off and let out a bark of laughter that sounded like a hyena. It spurred me on.

I won't let you use me! I'm not your pawn, your puppet to control! I clamped my mind shut, and was happy to see my uncle recoil.

"Why you little – !"

Raymond redoubled his efforts and probed deeper into my mind. *Shut it down! Shut it closed!* I chanted the old mantra. For a moment, I saw black. The pressure receded and faded away.

I opened my eyes, saw that my uncle wore a grimace of frustration.

"You're young, Gregory, and you're no match for me. Eventually I'll wear you down."

He turned and left the room, leaving me huddled in my chair. I rubbed my arms to warm the chill that had seeped into my body. It was stupid to let my guard down, to lose myself amid my emails and websites. I'd given my uncle a chance to get inside my head! What a sap!

No matter. It was the last time Raymond would make me his pawn. He was strong. I'd felt his power. But my own emerging powers would keep him at bay. I would practice what Lucinda had taught me until I mastered the art of keeping my mind closed.

I had to, if I wanted to survive.

Chapter Seven

I awoke the following morning, feeling tired and groggy. I considered calling the camp to say I was sick, but I was curious to know what Andy and Pol had to tell me. Besides, hanging around the house wasn't an option. What if Raymond came home, wanting to try another of his infusions?

I used the bathroom and got dressed, weighed down by a headache and memories belonging to my uncle: images of growing up in Buckley; an older man telling how his health improved minutes after snuffing out a young boy's life. I wondered if the boy was Lucinda's brother.

Another boy showed up in a series of scenes. It took me a minute to realize the boy was my father. Eddie featured in Raymond's most cherished memories of childhood: his teaching Eddie to ride a two-wheeler, to shoot a bow and arrow, to ski. When the brothers were thirteen and seventeen, Eddie and Raymond had a fierce argument. Eddie took a swing at Raymond. Raymond reached out to Eddie's head and held him off at arm's length, mocking him all the while. Eddie ran off, crying tears of fury.

Were they fighting about The Davenport Curse, as I called my relatives' fondness of draining a victim's vital essence to extend their own lives? It could very well be, because this was the last memory Raymond had left me of my father.

As I waited for the bus, I thought about how Dad had opposed the

Davenport's killings since he was a teenager. *My uncle didn't care that his younger brother left Buckley. Until he needed me.* I shivered, despite the sun beating down on my head and shoulders. How I wanted to leave this town and never come back! Then I remembered. My father had done that, and a lot of good it had done him, my mother, and Lucy.

At camp, I found myself manifesting a few of Raymond's personality traits. When two eight-year-old boys began to whine, claiming the water was too cold to swim, I didn't give them my usual lecture. Instead, I promised that if they stayed in for at least ten minutes, I'd buy them ice cream at lunch time. The boys remained in the water for the entire period.

"I want a popsicle," one boy shouted as he was drying off.

"And I want a cup of chocolate ice cream," the other said.

"They're yours," I promised as I watched them run off to get dressed. I certainly didn't mind buying them ice cream, but I didn't like the idea of bribing kids to swim. Besides, if word got out, I'd be treating half the camp to ice cream before the week was over.

Lunchtime I bought a sandwich and soda, then hurried over to the table I shared with Andy and Pol. I slid across from Pol, who was eating a cup of flavored yogurt.

"Hey, Pol. Where's Andy?"

Pol gestured with her spoon. "He's talking up our idea with some of the other kids. The more people get involved, the better chance we have of getting results."

Though her manner was blasé as usual, I picked up on her excitement. "What are you talking about?"

Pol shot me a look of disdain. "It's what we wanted to discuss with you last night. Andy and I realized it's up to us to stop your uncle from building condos on the playing fields."

My heart thundered in my chest as an internal voice ordered me not to tell Pol that construction would begin once the paperwork was in place. Instead, I was to learn everything I could about the twins' plans. A cold rage settled over me. I would not allow my uncle to control me!

Still, I didn't have to tell Pol about the condo plans right now. "What's next on the Save the Playing Fields campaign?"

"We're meeting tomorrow night to rally support to keep the playing fields as they are. Dad said he'd check out the legal papers, see if there's a loop hole we can use to hold up construction. Meanwhile, we'll draw up petitions, get as many Buckley residents to sign them. Dad's going to check if the city council can defeat the motion."

"With Uncle Raymond leading them on?" I scoffed. "I doubt it."

"You don't have to be so negative."

"I'm being honest."

Pol threw me a hurt look. "Are you with us or against us?"

The Raymond influence inside me urged me to cover my tracks. "What do you think?" I sputtered. "I'm with you, Pol. All the way."

Pol wrinkled her nose. "What's gotten into you?"

"What do you mean?"

"You're acting different lately. Downright strange."

Andy rushed over just then, saving me from answering. He sat across from me and tossed a list of names on the table. His cheeks were red; his eyes glittered with excitement.

"Eight people said they'll come tomorrow night. They're all bringing friends and relatives."

"Where's this meeting?" I asked.

"Our house." Andy put a sheet of paper in front of me. "Here's a petition form. Try to get as many people as you can to sign. Make sure they include addresses and phone numbers."

"Uh, I don't think it's a good idea for me to be doing this."

"Why not?" Andy asked.

"Are you kidding? My uncle will be furious if he hears I've been collecting signatures."

Pol and Andy exchanged glances. "I told you," Pol said.

Enough of my own personality was present to make me realize that if I didn't go along with this, I'd lose their friendship forever.

"I'll do it." I took the petition and folded it.

"Great!" Andy grinned, quick to forgive. "Just don't let your uncle see it, okay?"

"Of course." I bit into my tuna salad sandwich, though I was no longer hungry. My life was getting so complicated, I could hardly think straight.

"Excuse me, guys."

Startled, I jumped a foot in the air. I turned to see Craig Averil, hands on hips, standing behind me.

"I hate to interrupt your one free period of the day, but I was hoping one of you could do me a favor."

Andy eyed him warily. "What is it?"

"Both secretaries are out, and I need someone to cover the office." Craig flashed the toothy smile that made him such a hit with his female students. "Any one of you up for volunteering to man the phones for the rest of the lunch period?"

"Will the volunteer get paid extra?" Pol asked.

"I'll do it!" I offered before Craig had a chance to answer Pol's question.

"Wonderful!" Craig clapped a hand on my shoulder. "Gather up your lunch and follow me." He flashed Pol a smile. "For future information, volunteers get paid back with time off. Sorry, the budget doesn't allow for monetary remuneration."

I followed Craig through the lunchroom to the office at the front of the building. I breathed in the cool air and decided that sitting in an air-conditioned room was an unexpected bonus I hadn't counted on when I'd grabbed the chance to get away from Andy and Pol. The less I saw of them the better, until I decided how to deal with them.

The office was small, compact, and orderly, with not an inch of wasted space. Tall file cabinets stood along one wall. Craig pointed to one of the two facing desks in the center of the room. Each were large enough to hold a computer and a phone.

"Why don't you sit at Cheryl's desk and finish your lunch? When the phone rings, say, 'Good afternoon. Shady Brook Day Camp, Simon speaking,' and take a message."

I noted the pen and pad of paper next to the phone. "Sound's easy enough."

"We get very few calls in the middle of the day, but someone has to be here at all times. I've got a counselor covering next period, so you can leave at ten to one."

When Craig left, I finished eating my sandwich. I welcomed the solitude and the silence. The only sound was the air conditioner whirring and clicking off and on. The phone rang—a mother calling to say she was stopping at camp before two o'clock to bring over her daughter's bathing suit. I jotted down the message and ripped the sheet from the pad.

There was nothing to do, so I took out the petition. I read it and laughed. While I sympathized with the twins' cause, I doubted their efforts would get them anywhere. Raymond owned the playing fields property and the town had no legal standing. So why were they wasting everyone's time, mine included?

Irritated, I told myself I had more important things to think about. I had to figure out how to escape Raymond's clutches before the monster succeeded in taking over my body. Running away was no solution, unless…unless I could find Aunt Grace!

I stared at the computer, excitement surging through my body. I typed her name in the Google Directory. Her old address in New Mexico came up. I quickly deleted all traces of my search. I needed to hook up my cell phone with a service. Now that I had funds, I could do it myself. And this way Raymond couldn't track my calls.

I picked up the pencil and started a "to do" list: Put phone in service. Call Aunt Grace. Call Gretel. Visit L soon. I felt my spirits rising. I wasn't totally alone. Surely Lucinda would come up with a plan to help me.

I smiled as her words came back to me. "Remember, your power is greater than Raymond's." I hoped it was true. I *had* to believe it was true, if I was going to save my life.

I noticed the small radio on the book shelf, and listened to a music station. Finally, Brittany, one of the counselors, came in and said I could leave. I was stepping into the pool, ready to instruct the six-year-old girls, when I let out a gasp of horror. I'd left the petition on the desk, open for anyone to read.

Chapter Eight

As soon as I got home, I raced upstairs to get my smart phone, which I kept in the top drawer of my desk. I stared at it, amazed that I hadn't missed it until now. I took a check from the checkbook, and went looking for my aunt. I found her behind the house watering flowers.

"Aunt Mary, I'm going into town for a while."

"All right, Simon. Anything special you'd like for dinner tonight? Your uncle has a meeting, so it will be just the two of us."

I grinned. Terrific! No Raymond at the dinner table. "Anything's okay." A thought occurred to me. "How about hot dogs?"

Aunt Mary beamed at me. "That's a wonderful idea. I have baked beans and relish, but no buns. I'll pick some up when I'm in town." She shook her head in amazement. "I haven't had a hot dog since—since I can't remember when."

"Me, neither."

"Then we're long overdue," Aunt Mary said.

I walked the five blocks into town, thinking about my conversation with Aunt Mary. It was like any normal conversation with a relative. The kind we never had before. Why? I wondered. Probably because she usually acted like a zombie, probably from all the pills she took. Did she know about her husband's ungodly behavior? She had to. After all, she'd lived with Raymond all these years.

Then why didn't she get away? Probably for the same reason I wasn't running. There was no escape.

A chill ran down my back. Maybe Aunt Mary was in cahoots with my uncle, the two of them working hand in hand. Maybe her job was to throw me off guard so Raymond would have an easier time breaking down my defenses.

Reactivating my smart phone account was easier than I'd expected. I told the college-aged salesman to send me the bill via email so it wouldn't arrive in the mail. The less Raymond knew about my business, the better. That taken care of, I walked up the block and dropped onto one of the benches outside the library. I took out the scrap of paper on which I'd jotted down my aunt's phone number and thumbed the tiny pads.

"This number is no longer in service."

I frowned. Still? Where was Aunt Grace? I shuddered. Had something happened to her, too? No, that was too crazy. There was no reason why my uncle would harm my mother's sister.

I retrieved the "Gretel" number from my shorts' pocket and made the call. A tingle ran up my back as I waited.

"Who is this?" a man with a gruff voice asked.

Startled, I blurted out my name.

"Finally." He let out a deep sigh. "Are you alone?"

I glanced around. Two teenaged girls in tennis whites whom I recognized as seniors, a grade ahead of me, stood laughing and chatting near the library entrance, well out of hearing range.

"I'm alone. Who are you? Why did you send me an email?"

"Because I have vital information for you. Christ! I didn't think you'd take this long to call. She's frantic with worry."

"Who's frantic with worry? Who are you?"

"Listen, Simon, all I can do is pass on a phone number to you, which I hope and pray you call ASAP. Believe me, you'll be glad you did."

50

"What's with the Gretel business?"

"I've no idea what you're talking about."

I drew a deep breath and let it out. "Is this about my sister?"

"Here's the number. Got a pen?"

"No. Wait!" I shouted because he was rattling off a long distance number. He let out an exaggerated sigh of exasperation. "Hurry up. Get with it, kid."

I ran over to the two girls. "Do either of you have a pen I can borrow?"

The pretty, dark-haired girl opened her small purse. "Sure. Here you go."

"I'll bring it right back," I promised. I raced back to the bench. "I've got a pen now."

The man repeated the number and I wrote it carefully on the back of the slip of paper. "Don't lose it," he warned. "Now that we've made contact, this number's going to disconnect."

He hung up, and I started to giggle. Made contact? This number's going to disconnect? It was like something out of "Mission Impossible." What was the guy smoking? For all I knew, this could turn out to be one huge prank. But who would go through the trouble of carrying out a prank like this? Besides, the email had been sent back in May. Almost two months ago.

The tall blonde girl must have left, because the brunette was alone when I handed back her pen. "Keep it," she said, flashing a bright smile. "I've a drawer full of them at home."

"Thanks." She had a dynamite bod, I noticed, and a great tan.

"You're new to Buckley, aren't you?"

"Kind of. I moved here in April. My name's Simon Porte."

She surprised me by holding out her hand. "Tasha Wells. I've seen you around."

I shook her hand, surprised by the firmness of her grip.

"And I've seen you. You're a cheerleader, right?"

She winked, suddenly looking elfish and full of mischief. "Don't let that scare you off."

I grinned. "Okay, I won't."

Tasha glanced down at the books she was holding. "I'd better get going. Want a lift anywhere?"

"No, thanks. I have to take care of something."

Tasha opened her eyes in mock surprise. "Sounds very mysterious."

"Actually, it is mysterious."

"Maybe you'll tell me about it some time."

"Maybe I will," I answered, flustered by her attention. Was Tasha Wells interested in me or was this how she came on to every guy? And what was I doing, talking to a girl when I had to make an important phone call? "Gotta go," I called over my shoulder as I took off in the direction of the adjoining park.

My fingers trembled as I dialed the new number. Another male voice answered, only this guy was more polite.

"Hello, who is this, please?"

"Simon Porte."

A pause, then, "Can you verify that?"

"Sure. How?"

"What's your mother's maiden name?"

"Cassidy."

"Your sister's birthday."

I swallowed. "May sixteenth."

"What did you give her for her last birthday?"

"A Barbie doll dressed in a gown."

"Call this number in an hour. It may ring several times. Wait until someone answers."

"Okay."

The man read off a telephone number with a different area code and had me repeat it back to him. He hung up.

An hour! Jeez. An hour from now I'd be eating dinner. I worried as I headed for home. How was I going to keep this from Raymond? Then I remembered my uncle wasn't going to be home dinner time. I'd tell Aunt Mary I wasn't feeling well so I could make the call from my bedroom.

But when I got home, I found Aunt Mary more excited than I'd ever seen her.

"I bought buns, potato salad, and cole slaw to go with our hot dogs. And I'll cut up a nice tomato salad with some fresh basil. How does that sound?"

She looked so happy, so pleased with all her dinner preparations, I didn't have the heart to carry out my plan. I came up with another idea.

"Sounds terrific, Aunt Mary, but do you think we could eat early tonight? I'm meeting Andy and Pol earlier than usual. We've got some things to take care of."

"Of course, Simon. Why don't you set the table right now?" She smiled mischievously. "And we'll use paper plates, something your uncle Raymond doesn't approve of." Her face took on an anxious expression. "I hope you don't mind my making the hot dogs on the stove. Your uncle always does the barbecuing, and I'm afraid to handle the grill."

I opened my mouth to offer to start the grill, then closed it. "Stove top franks will be fine, Aunt Mary." And faster, too.

We sat down to dinner twenty minutes later. For the first time since I'd moved to Buckley, I felt totally at ease in my aunt and uncle's home. Aunt Mary surprised me by talking up a storm about her childhood.

"I met Raymond when I was your age – fifteen," she said, a faraway look in her eyes. "It was spring time. May, to be exact. Our two churches got together to have a dance for all the young folk."

"Are you from Buckley?" I asked.

"From Chatham Falls. That's west of here, about ten miles away."

"Melissa Gordon's from Chatham Falls," I said.

Aunt Mary shook her head. "Poor child. May she rest in peace."

I remained silent, hoping she'd say more. Finally, she shook her head again, and added, "I know her mother. Knew her when we were young. She's my friend Cynthia's baby sister. I can't imagine what she must be suffering."

Suffering caused by Raymond! Did Aunt Mary know her husband had killed the little girl? She *had* to know. I wondered if Aunt Mary was suddenly so chatty because my uncle had told her to soften me up. Make me more vulnerable. More malleable. Well, two could play that game. I decided it was time I started asking questions.

"Why didn't you and Uncle Raymond have children?"

Aunt Mary's eyes misted over, and she gave me a sad smile. "Unfortunately, it wasn't meant to be. I had certain difficulties when we first married." She sighed. "I overcame them a few years later, but then Raymond took sick. He grew weaker and weaker. For a while we had an aide coming to the house every day." She smiled at me. "At last, he began to get well. Then he brought you home and got an entirely new lease on life."

"I bet," I mumbled.

Aunt Mary patted my arm. "No, really. I know he's caught up in his business dealings and doesn't always know how to treat a teenaged boy who's practically a young man, but his heart's in the right place."

I couldn't bear to hear another word. I bolted from the table and dropped off my dish to the sink. "Thanks, Aunt Mary. Dinner was great. Gotta go."

"But you didn't have dessert!" she exclaimed. "I bought an apple tart for you in the bakery."

"I'll eat it when I get home." I bent down to kiss her cheek. "Bye, Aunt Mary. See you later."

Was she for real? I wondered as I jogged toward the elementary school. Could she be that naïve and totally clueless regarding Raymond's crimes? I remembered how sad she'd looked the other day, how I'd sensed she was feeling bad for me.

Unless she was in on it and her husband's accomplice! Maybe Aunt Mary's job was to convince me she was harmless so I wouldn't be on my guard when she helped spring a trap. Was Uncle Raymond planning a transformation for Aunt Mary, too? Or was he leaving Aunt Mary behind?

It was seven o'clock when I got to the school yard. Though I didn't expect the twins to arrive until eight – if they showed up that evening – I wasn't taking any chances. Four boys were playing a fast game of basketball on the court a good five hundred feet away. I sat down on the steps leading to one of the side entrances and dialed the last number I'd been given.

"Hello?" A woman's voice. It sounded like Aunt Grace's voice, but I couldn't be sure.

"Aunt Grace?"

"Who is this?"

"It's Simon."

"Finally!" she said, relief and laughter spilling over the line. "We've been waiting to hear from you for months. I was at my wits' end."

"I didn't have access to my computer or my phone until yesterday." I hesitated, then asked, "This is Aunt Grace, right?"

"Of course it's me, Simon. I'm so glad to be speaking to you."

A thousand questions flooded my mind, but I could ask only one at a time. "Where were you when my parents and Lucy were killed? I know my parents had you down in their wills as our legal guardian, but the police couldn't find you."

"I know, dear. I'm awfully sorry about that, but it couldn't be helped."

"Why not?"

Her silence pulsed with fear and anxiety. "Where are you, Simon? Can anyone hear your part of this conversation?"

I grimaced. "No. Is all this secrecy because of my uncle?"

"Yes, Simon." She paused, then asked, "Has he harmed you?"

I didn't want to upset her further, so I skirted the truth. "I'm all right, though the man's demented."

"I'm sorry I wasn't able to come get you, but after the accident I had to follow your parents' instructions if I was to keep Lucy safe."

My head began to spin. My breath come in deep gasps. "Lucy? You're saying she's alive?"

Aunt Grace laughed. "Very much so, and wanting to speak to her brother."

I swallowed, too dazed to speak. Lucy was alive! When I found my voice again, I asked, "Lucy's with you?"

"Right here. Hold on a second."

My heart thumped as I waited. A minute later, the familiar voice I knew and loved so well sounded in my ear.

"Hi Sy-sy"

"Hello, Lu-lu."

"Where are you?" Lucy asked. "I miss you so much."

"I'm in Buckley, New York. And I miss you, too."

"When can you get here?" Lucy asked.

"Very soon. Where are you?"

There were scraping sounds. My aunt returned to the phone. "We can't tell you where we are, Simon. It isn't safe."

I blinked, trying to absorb what my aunt was saying. "Why can't I come live with you and Lucy? I want us to be together."

"I know you do, dear, but I can't take the risk. Your Uncle Raymond's a monster who preys on girls Lucy's age." Her breath caught. "Even speaking to you is an awful risk. He has people working for him, people who stop at nothing." She tried to stifle her sobs, but I knew she was

CHAPTER EIGHT

crying. "Look what they did to your poor parents."

Here was the confirmation, if I had any lingering doubts. It felt like someone had punched me in the chest. "When can I talk to Lucy again?"

"I don't know, Simon. Maybe not for a while. Please don't call this number again. I'll be changing it tomorrow."

"But, Aunt Grace – " The phone went dead.

Chapter Nine

I covered my face with my hands, as hot tears streamed down my cheeks. Lucy was alive! Aunt Grace was looking after her, but she wouldn't let me come live with them. No, I had to stay here in Buckley with my awful devil of an uncle and his diabolical plan to take over my body. It wasn't fair!

Life isn't fair. So my father had told me when I'd lost the spelling bee because my word was ten times harder than the one the winner had to spell. When I'd twisted my ankle days before the most important meet of ninth grade. "Life isn't fair," Dad used to say, "but we do the best we can, given the circumstances. And in this case, the circumstances were that Lucy had to remain safe and out of our uncle's clutches.

I sniffed, furious for having wasted energy feeling sorry for myself. I ran through my conversation with Aunt Grace. Then I sat back and considered what she'd said—and what she'd left out.

She must have met my parents that night if she'd managed to get Lucy before they were killed. Were my parents planning to take me with them, wherever they intended to go? Or—it suddenly occurred to me—they were going to drive to Toronto, to leave me with Mom's college roommate.

I bet Aunt Grace could tell me what had sent my parents fleeing, and where they had intended to go. She'd told the authorities that Lucy had been in the car in order to protect her from Raymond. The one article I'd read said Lucy's body must have fallen into a snow-covered ravine and couldn't be retrieved until spring. I grimaced. At the time, I hadn't the heart to read more about it, though I should have.

My parents must have been terrified, knowing Raymond was hunting them down. They thought they were protecting me by keeping me in the dark about the Davenport's history. I'd have been better prepared if I had known.

I longed to see Lucy. If I could tweak her braids, hear her giggle at my silly jokes again, I'd know there were some good things left in this world. It was just the two of us now. It was my responsibility to educate her about important things, like how to deal with boys.

I'd figure out a way to see her, whether Aunt Grace approved or not.

Great-Aunt Lucinda could help me find Lucy! I stood, ready to head over to her house, when I remembered I had to contact her first in case someone was spying on me. On both of us. Damn all this spying and hiding! I was thoroughly sick of it!

At any rate, the twins were expecting me. Meeting with a bunch of kids who had no chance of changing Raymond's mind about the playing fields was the last thing I wanted to do, but I couldn't back out. I had an obligation to support Andy and Pol. The twins were the only friends I had, and I didn't want to alienate them. They were already put off by my lack of interest. I'd stay a while then contact Lucinda.

Darkness fell as I jogged over to their house. Lights, muted by gauzy drapes, shone from the downstairs windows. A wave of longing for my own home and my own family swept over me. I wiped away the tears that filled my eyes and rang the doorbell.

Pol opened the door. "Hey, Simon. I'm glad you decided to come tonight."

Annoyed, I said, "Told you I'd be here, didn't I?"

I followed her into the den, where chairs had been set up for the meeting. Three boys and two girls, fellow camp counselors and classmates, chatted as they munched on chips and nuts.

Andy caught my eye and hurried over. "Yo, Simon. Did you get a lot of signatures? I've more sheets if you need them."

"Signatures?" For a moment, I had no idea what he was talking about.

"Come on, man! Get with it!" Andy shook his head in despair.

"Oh, right. The petition. I only got a few names so far, but I can use another sheet."

"Really?" Andy broke out into a grin. He poked the boy closest to him in the ribs. "Hear that, Ken? We've got Davenport's own nephew on our side."

The doorbell rang and Pol went to answer it. Three more kids joined the group. By the time Andy called the meeting to order, there were sixteen of us all together.

I leaned back in my chair by the fireplace, impressed by Andy's gift of leadership. He gave an upbeat introduction to the reason for the meeting, then had us introduce ourselves. This led to a lively discussion that he managed to control without hurting anyone's ego. Pol collected the petitions a few had managed to fill, and asked who needed more forms. I took one, feeling bad for my deception. I had no intention of getting any signatures, but I needed to give the impression that I was involved. If I didn't show an interest in their project, Andy and Pol would turn their backs on me.

Andy read off a list of people in the community who supported keeping the playing fields for sporting activities. He stressed how important it was to get as many signatures as possible.

"You've done great, bringing in almost three hundred names, but we need at least a thousand by the next city council meeting, which is in two weeks. We need to make the council view this is a serious issue for the town. We have to show them we have right on our side."

Andy's friend, Ken, a skinny boy with acne, grumbled something about my uncle. It must have been scuzzy, because the kids sitting near him giggled. When Ken caught me looking at him, he flushed and turned away.

"Did your dad speak to a lawyer yet?" I asked.

"Yes," Pol said. "Mr. Bayard is looking into it for us. He said it's going to take some time because he needs to find the deed to the land and the document detailing the town's use of the land."

"You mean they're missing?" a girl exclaimed.

The room buzzed with comments.

Andy frowned. "It's not so much that they're missing as they're not easy to locate. The documents are over a hundred years old. There was a fire in the records room in the Sixties, and all the old papers got dumped together. It could take some time before they find them."

If they find them. The kids were so naïve. I felt sorry for them. My uncle was an astute businessman. I had no doubt that he possessed a copy of the deed to the property as well as any document outlining the town's permission to use the property.

I grew restless and eager to leave. I had to speak to Great-Aunt Lucinda! I stood when Andy had his back to me, heatedly explaining how civic responsibility made a difference to one of the girls who was losing interest in the project.

I was surprised when Pol followed me outside.

"Well, good night," I said, eager to be on my way.

Pol nudged my shoulder. "You didn't collect any signatures." It was a statement, not a question.

I opted for the truth. "Nope."

"Something's going down with you, something big."

I met the intense gaze of her blue-green eyes. Again I decided not to lie. "Something huge, but nothing I can talk about."

Pol studied me in the shadow cast by the overhead light. It felt like she was peering into my soul. She treated me to one of her rare smiles that lit up her face. "Any time you want to spill what's on your mind, let me know. I'm a great listener."

"Thanks. I appreciate that."

I waved and started jogging back toward the school yard. No one else was in the street, but I didn't feel lonesome. The hard shell that had protected my heart these last few months was melting. I felt warm and cozy, the way I'd felt sitting in front of the fireplace after a day out on the ski slopes. Pol was all right. She was nobody's fool, as my mother would say. She was a good friend, regardless of how many signatures I brought in or didn't.

She was my ally.

When the elementary school came into view, I headed for the side entrance where I'd sat speaking to Lucy and Aunt Grace earlier in the evening. I had to talk to Lucinda. She had psychic powers. Maybe she could tell me where Aunt Grace had taken Lucy.

Aunt Grace didn't want me to join them, but that was because she had no idea what Raymond intended to do to me. Surely, she'd take me in once I explained the danger I was in and let me stay. Lucy needed me. I needed Lucy if I was going to keep my sanity and escape Raymond's diabolical plan.

I closed my eyes and repeated the numbers: 4-8-6-1. 4-8-6-1. 4-8-6-1. I repeated it again and again in my mind.

"Enough already!" Lucinda's irritated voice resounded in my head. "I hear you. I hear you!"

I laughed aloud, delighted to have connected with Lucinda so easily. I opened my mouth to speak, then realized I only had to think the words.

"This is better than owning a Blue Tooth."

"A blue tooth? What kind of strange objects do you kids come up with these days?"

"Forget it. Aunt Lucinda, I gotta see you right away."

"Come by the house. Keep an eye out for spies, but I don't sense that anyone's following you tonight."

"I wonder if anyone followed me to the meeting at the twins' house. They're organizing opposition to Uncle Raymond's condo plan."

"Tell me about it when you get here."

I looked around before setting out for Lucinda's cottage. Though it was dark out, I saw everything as clearly as if it were daylight. I heard cats and other creatures prowling around lawns, caught snatches of TV dialogue coming from the houses I passed. My hearing was keener now, as was my sight. Lucinda was right! My uncle's infusions were sharpening my senses. I'd have to work at closing myself to random sights and sounds, but right now they served an excellent purpose.

Lucinda greeted me with a hug and led me into the kitchen. My aunt's home felt familiar, as though I were a frequent visitor and this wasn't my second time here.

"It's like I've always known you," I said as she placed a glass of milk and a piece of apple cake before me.

Lucinda patted my shoulder. "That's because we're kin. God knows you deserve to have a relative who cares about your well being."

I looked up at her. "I spoke to Lucy! She's alive, but our Aunt Grace won't let me come live with them. You have to help me, Lucinda!"

"Whoa!" Lucinda stuck out her palm. She dropped into a chair and faced me. "Start over, Simon. Slowly."

I drew a deep breath and explained how I'd managed to contact Aunt Grace and how Lucy and I needed to be together. "We can't even talk, Aunt Lucinda, because Aunt Grace keeps on changing the phone numbers. You have to help us! I know you can."

Lucinda pressed her lips together. She looked dead serious. "Remember that girl you told me about – Melissa Gordon?"

I nodded.

"Another little girl was killed this evening. It was on the radio."

My pulse began to race. "That lousy, dirty —"

"She was nine years old. Lucy's age."

I blinked. "But Lucy's his niece!"

"Meaning her life force is the strongest, most premium kind of fuel for Raymond." Lucinda grimaced. "Don't forget my brother. My grandfather killed him."

I wouldn't give up. I couldn't. "I'd be careful not to leave a trail of where I was going. Aunt Grace managed to keep Lucy hidden all these months."

"You mustn't try to see Lucy! Don't contact her. Your aunt is keeping her safe. She knows what she's up against. Raymond would come after you – twice as fast and twice as hard – if he knew Lucy was alive."

"But how would he know?"

Lucinda turned away. "He'd find out somehow."

Her words defeated me. I was alone again. Only now it was worse because I couldn't join my sister. "I thought you'd help me get away from here. I want to stay with Aunt Grace and live with Lucy." My voice broke. "You've no idea how hard it's been for me."

Lucinda came to stand behind my chair. She wrapped her arms around me. They were bony, but comforting.

"You have to be strong a while longer. We'll defeat your awful uncle. Then you and Lucy can be together."

I turned to face her. "How? How are we supposed to defeat this devil who kills and controls and means to turn me into a zombie!"

"We're working on it. Have you been practicing closing your mind?"

"Yes."

"Keep at it. Day and night. Have there been more infusions?"

"One." I snorted. "But Raymond didn't find it much of a success."

"Good. That proves how strong you are."

"He's powerful, Aunt Lucinda."

"You're stronger," she insisted. "Keep practicing your closing skills. Soon you'll be able to do it in your sleep."

"I have some of his memories. I kind of know how he works things so they go his way."

Lucinda sent me a sharp look of concern. "Don't let it go any further."

"Right." Like I could control what was happening to me. I stood and let out an enormous yawn. It had been a long day. "I'd better get going." Absentmindedly, I slipped my hand in my pocket and pulled out the folded petition form Andy had given me.

"What's that?" Lucinda asked.

I explained, and was puzzled by the huge grin that wreathed her wrinkled cheeks.

"What's so funny, Aunt Lucinda?"

She was laughing so hard, for a minute she couldn't answer. "Your Uncle Raymond, that's what. I can't wait to see his face when we put a stop to his precious condo plans."

Chapter Ten

I gaped at Lucinda. Maybe she really was going senile.

"Simon, dear, you're talking about the land behind the shops on Elm Street?"

"Yeah. The town uses it for Little League and soccer games. Four games can be in play at the same time."

"Beyond it there's a stretch of woods?"

"There are houses there. No woods, I don't think."

"Of course! My grandfather sold off that parcel of property. He needed the money at the time."

"I don't see how you can stop Raymond from building his condos?" I yawned again.

"Simon, that property – where the kids play baseball and what-have-you – is Davenport land. It belongs to all of us, not just Raymond. That includes you, me, and Lucy, for that matter."

Excitement coursed through me. I was no longer tired. "Really? You mean, Uncle Raymond has no right to build condos on that property?"

"Not without our say-so. Though, judging by his actions, he doesn't see it that way."

"Do you have a copy of the deed?"

"I should." She blinked. "Let's see, It's somewhere in the spare bedroom. Or maybe in my safety deposit box. Or did I give it to my lawyer to keep in his safe?"

I felt a stab of disappointment. "Don't you know where it is?"

"Not offhand."

"We need that deed, Aunt Lucinda!"

"Don't badger me, Simon. I promise you I'll find it. Now go home and get some sleep. I'm growing weary myself. And practice closing your mind. Practice, practice, practice."

I walked home in a funk. I'd counted on Lucinda's help to find Lucy. Instead, she'd told me not to talk to her if I wanted to keep her safe from Raymond. But Lucinda wasn't concerned that Raymond was out to destroy me! Oh, no. She insisted I was stronger than Raymond!

The situation was a disaster, and I didn't know what to do. I kicked a rock and sent it flying across the road. Meanwhile, Raymond went on killing little girls and making plans to build condos. Raymond could do whatever he liked, whenever he liked, and no one had the power to stop him.

I unlocked the front door and entered the dimly lit hall. Raised voices were coming from my uncle's office. At first I thought it was the television. Then I realized my aunt and uncle were arguing.

I pressed my ear against the door and listened.

Aunt Mary was sobbing. "I will not, I cannot help you any longer!"

"You must, Mary. You promised when we got married."

"That was before I knew what you and your family were about."

"Oh, you knew all right!" Raymond sounded angry. "You knew when I paid off your father's mortgage on the farm."

"Yes, I found out when it was too late!" Aunt Mary retorted. "I was horrified. It was too late for me, but I promised myself I'd never bear your child."

"You did what!"

"You're a monster, Raymond. Did you think I'd bring your kind into the world?"

She laughed hysterically. There was the sound of a smack, then silence.

"Go to sleep," Raymond said softly. "You will forget this argument and remember your promise to help me with my plans."

"Yes, Raymond," Aunt Mary answered meekly.

"You will be kind to Simon but show your allegiance to me, your husband."

"Yes, Raymond."

My God, he's been hypnotizing her! No wonder she's a zombie half the time.

The office door opened. I flew upstairs as Aunt Mary came into the hall. I raced to my room and slammed the door shut, wishing I could erase the awful scene from my head. My spirits sank below basement level because I had no one to help me. Aunt Lucinda was dotty. Aunt Mary was under Raymond's spell. There wasn't an adult in all of Buckley I could count on. I fell into bed and closed my eyes. The only person I could rely on was myself! I'd figure out a way to escape and get to Lucy, if it was the last thing I did.

I washed up and put on my pajamas, wondering if I'd have to undergo another of my uncle's infusion sessions. God, when would this day end?

I lay in the dark and practiced closing my mind. When the half-expected knock came minutes later, I barely reacted. "Come in."

"Simon," Raymond said, "I was hoping you were still awake."

"I am."

"Do you mind switching on your lamp?"

Does it matter if I mind? "Sure, Uncle Raymond."

My uncle held out a sheet of paper folded in quarters. "I believe this is yours."

My heart raced as I stared down at the paper. It was the petition Andy had given me at lunch time. *What should I say?* I ran through several responses in my head and grinned when I'd decided how I to play this.

I handed the petition back to Raymond. "What about it?"

"Is it yours?"

"Looks like it's yours now. I suppose Craig Averil gave it to you. Did you tell him to spy on me?

My insolence rattled him, but not for long. "When I saw Mr. Averil this evening, he mentioned you'd worked in his office today and must have left this on his desk. He asked me to return it to you."

I laughed. "Great recovery, unc. I'm impressed."

Raymond pursed his lips. "I'd like to remind you I'm your uncle and you are to show me respect."

I felt the push of his psychic force and closed my mind just in time. I watched him recoil, a stunned expression on his face. Maybe Lucinda was right, and I was stronger than Raymond.

"And how shall I do that—show you respect?"

"By answering my questions with a civil tongue." Raymond rattled the paper in my face. "Who gave you this petition?"

I had no wish to make the twins the object of my uncle's fury, but the news of their activities was bound to get out. In fact, Raymond probably knew all about their meeting by now.

"Andy Coltrane handed it to me during lunch." I shrugged. "I explained I couldn't get signatures since I don't know anything about those playing fields."

Raymond looked relieved. "They can collect all the signatures they like, but it won't do them any good. I own the property."

I met his gaze. "*You* do?"

Raymond's eyes slid away. "Who else?"

I shrugged. "Just asking. Can I go to sleep now?"

Raymond studied me. I stared back at him. *Just try one of your infusions!*

But my uncle had other things on his mind. "Tomorrow, instead of coming straight home from camp, I'd like you to meet me in town – at our lawyers' office."

My pulse went into overdrive. "Why? What's wrong?"

Raymond reached out to pat my arm. I had to exert a burst of self-control not to yank free.

"Nothing's wrong. We've a few legal matters to settle. I didn't want to bother you with them when you first came to live with us, but they need attending. Can you get on a camp bus that will drop you off in town? The address is 154 Main Street. Garrison and Bergson. They're on the second floor. Here's their card." Raymond placed it on my dresser. "Our appointment's at four thirty."

Now what was he after? Regardless of what it was, it couldn't be good. "Okay. I'll be there," I agreed, knowing I had no choice but to play dumb.

My uncle rewarded me with a broad smile. "Good boy. In fact, I'll be changing my will. I'm leaving everything to you."

The kiss of death! He's leaving me his money because he intends to become me. I wanted to jump out of bed and run out of the house. Instead, I said, "Thanks, Uncle Raymond. That's very kind of you."

"Don't mention it. Now go to sleep and get some rest. You've a big day ahead of you."

To my relief, he left and closed the door behind him.

Chapter Eleven

"What's the name of that lawyer who's looking into the playing fields property deed?" I asked the twins the next day at lunch. It had rained in the morning, so we were eating inside.

Andy finished chewing the huge bite of his hero sandwich and swallowed.

"Chuck Bayard. Why?"

My new rule of friendship: lie and share as little as possible. "I may need a lawyer," I said, going for casual.

Judging by the way Pol's mouth popped open, I hadn't succeeded. She glanced around the noisy lunchroom, and must have decided to hold all questions till later.

"Chuck's a junior partner in a large Albany firm. They have a small office here in town. He's real smart." She grinned. "And easy on the eyes."

Why the comment about his looks? And why would I care? I could use a smart lawyer," I said. "Got his number?"

"Andy has it on his cell phone." She looked meaningfully at her brother. "Give it to Simon."

Andy was dying to ask me why I needed a lawyer, but he obeyed Pol's message to keep his mouth shut. He sighed as he fished his phone from his pocket. He rattled off the number, and I added it to my list of contacts. Then I stood and tossed my half-eaten sandwich in the garbage. "Thanks. See you later."

Outside, I found a quiet spot at the rear of the building and called the lawyer. A secretary answered and asked me to hold. I smiled. So far, so good.

When Chuck Bayard picked up, I introduced himself, adding that I'd gotten his number from Andy. Then I explained why I needed an attorney.

"I'm meeting my uncle at his lawyer's office, and he's probably going to ask me to sign papers I've no intention of signing."

"Is your uncle your guardian?" Chuck asked.

"No, and I don't want him to be."

"Then the court will have to provide you with one. Is there another adult – preferably a relative – you'd rather live with?"

Aunt Grace was the logical choice, but God knew where she was at this moment. She certainly wasn't available to me. Great-Aunt Lucinda? She was too—flaky? Old?

"Offhand, I can't think of anyone. What will happen then? Would I stay in my uncle's house?"

"I can't say. A lot depends on the Family Court judge."

"Oh." *Another dead end. How can this lawyer help me when he knows zilch about me and my situation? He'd think I was nuts if I told him what Uncle Raymond's doing to me and those little girls.*

"Hey, Simon," Chuck finally said. "Why don't I pick you up from camp and drive you to the meeting? This will give us a chance to talk. I need to know everything you can tell me about your situation before I can offer you legal advice."

"Sounds like a good idea." I heard footsteps, turned and saw Craig Averil walking toward me. "Gotta go."

"Whoa, there! I know where the camp is. What time shall I pick you up?"

"Four's good. Wait for me on the road a hundred feet below where the buses line up."

"Got it. See you later."

I slipped my phone into my pocket and waited. Craig's expression of concern was as phony as a three dollar bill. I barely managed to suppress a shudder. This man was in my uncle's pay. For all I knew, he'd driven my parents off the road. How had Raymond convinced him to commit murder? Did he promise him money? How many millions was it worth to sell your soul to become the devil's henchman?

"I looked for you in the lunchroom," Craig said. "Everything all right?"

"I had to take care of something. Is there a problem?"

"No problem. Your Uncle Raymond called to remind you to take the bus that passes through town. It's number 8. Jenny Barnett's the driver."

"Thanks, Craig." I started walking toward the entrance of the rec hall.

"Simon."

I stopped and turned around. Craig closed the gap between us.

"I hope you're not angry because I gave your uncle the petition you'd left in the office."

I shrugged. "It doesn't matter."

"The truth is, I felt a conflict of loyalty – toward an old friend and toward a member of my staff."

Anger churned the bit of lunch I'd managed to eat into bile. I glared at Craig. "Where's the conflict? You work for my uncle and I work for you. I'll do my job in camp. Just keep away from me."

"Don't take that tone with me!"

My fury solidified into a molten ball of lava. I envisioned shooting it straight at Craig's gut. I thought I was hallucinating when Craig moaned and clutched his stomach.

"Or you'll do what?" I asked softly.

He straightened up and fled.

What have I done? What am I becoming? My joy at having bested Craig Averil faded away and I felt like a freak. Was what had happened the result of my uncle's infusions? Or were my own powers growing, developing faster than I could manage?

* * *

"There's not much to tell," I began as soon as Chuck Bayard U-turned and drove us away from the camp. "My parents died in an accident. My Aunt Grace was nowhere to be found, so they put me in foster care. Then my Uncle Raymond found me and brought me to Buckley."

"Quite a story," Chuck said thoughtfully.

I could see why girls would find him sexy. He was clean-cut, lean, and fit. I bet he'd run on the track team in high school and college. And he had a pleasant scent. Lately, I was picking up everyone's scent. Something else I had to work at blocking out.

"But why do I get the feeling you're leaving all the good parts out?"

And he was smart. I decided to offer a half-truth.

"My uncle's making me his heir. I'm worried he's doing this so, in exchange, I'll sign over my rights to the property now being used as the playing fields. According to my Great-Aunt Lucinda, all Davenports own equal parts of the property."

Chuck whistled. "That's news. I've been looking everywhere for the deed. Does you aunt have a copy of it?"

"She says she has it somewhere. I'm sure my uncle has his copy. Or his lawyer does."

Chuck stopped at a red light and gave me a searching look. "I get the impression you don't like your uncle very much."

I made a face. "You got that right."

"Lots of people don't like Raymond Davenport. But he's pretty powerful and well-connected. He's friends with everyone who's anyone in Buckley."

"Don't I know it," I grumbled.

Chuck laughed. "I didn't point that out to make you feel bad. Stay positive. I've a few connections of my own."

We parked and entered a building of professional suites. Uncle Raymond's lawyers had the entire third floor. Chuck let out a low whistle as we approached the receptionist's desk. "Marble, no less."

A gray-haired man with a moustache, dressed in a three-piece suit, came out to greet us. He smiled and shook hands with me. "Nice to meet you. I'm Paul Garrison, one of your uncle's lawyers." He blinked at Chuck, then quickly added, "I see you've brought a friend."

Chuck extended his hand, giving the other lawyer no choice but to shake it. "Chuck Bayard, with Terrance and Fine. I'm Mr. Porte's attorney."

"Oh! We weren't expecting...." Mr. Garrison gave off a whiff of fear. *What was he afraid of?* "Come this way," he said to me. "Your Uncle Raymond's waiting for you in the conference room."

Raymond and a heavyset man in his sixties were laughing heartily at a joke one of them had just told. I could tell they were old pals. Another person on my uncle's side. I was suddenly feeling vulnerable and was glad I'd brought Chuck along, if only for moral support.

Like Mr. Garrison, Raymond wasn't happy to see Chuck. *Good!* I thought. But my small boost of pleasure was washed away when he introduced the portly gentleman as Judge Arnold Potter. "He's a Family Court judge," Raymond explained. "Since Judge Potter wasn't holding court this afternoon, I asked him to attend our meeting, given the legal matters we have to discuss today."

Chuck and I took seats at the long table opposite Raymond and the judge. Paul Garrison sat at the head.

"What exactly are these legal matters to be discussed?" Chuck asked. "My client is concerned because he has no previous knowledge of them."

"That's because they're nothing but formalities," my uncle said. "Simon, you had no need to bring your own lawyer." He gave a false laugh. "Mr. Garrison is capable of representing us both."

"Only if your interests and Simon's are one and the same," Chuck said. "We've yet to find out if they are."

Raymond's eyes blazed with fury. "Now see here, young man! I've no intention of defrauding my nephew of one single penny of his inheritance! In fact, I've just revised my will and made him my sole heir."

Judge Potter placed a hand on my uncle's arm. "Easy does it, Raymond. You don't want to bring on a coronary."

"Shall we begin?" Mr. Garrison suggested. He turned to me. "Simon, feel free to stop me whenever you have a question, if you want me to explain a term or situation, or simply if you disagree. Okay?"

"Okay."

"And I'll advise my client when something's not in his best interest," Chuck added.

"Of course," Paul Garrison said smoothly. He glanced down at his notes, while Raymond glared at Chuck. "The first topic is Simon's guardianship." Mr. Garrison smiled at me. "Your uncle loves you and would like to be more than your guardian. He wants to adopt you, Simon, as well as make you his heir."

My heart began to pound. "I don't want to be adopted." I shot a look at my uncle. "No offense, Uncle Raymond, but my parents left it in their will that if they were to die, my mother's sister, Grace Addison, is to be my guardian."

Mr. Garrison sighed. "Your uncle has made every effort to find your aunt. She's left her home with no forwarding address. We've no way of contacting her."

Thank God for that! "Maybe she went off to Europe," I said. "She does that sometimes."

"In the meantime, your Aunt Mary and I have been caring for you as if you were our own son," Raymond said stiffly. "We thought you were aware of how much we love having you in our home."

I grimaced. "I appreciate your taking me into your home, but can't we go on as we've been? I mean, can't I live with you without being adopted?"

Raymond and the judge exchanged glances. The vibes they gave off sent a shiver down my spine. Judge Potter cleared his throat. "It's to your advantage to be declared your uncle's legal ward, Simon."

"Why?' Chuck asked. He grinned. "Does Simon's uncle intend to toss him out if he won't agree to the adoption? Is there some legal issue Mr. Davenport hopes to circumvent by having himself declared Simon's official guardian?"

Yay! I looked down to hide my grin while my uncle frowned at Chuck. Raymond didn't like this young lawyer defending my rights, which I bet had plenty to do with the playing fields property.

I suddenly had the need to say what was on my mind. To let my uncle know that I knew what he was after. "In a few years I'll be eighteen and considered an adult. I don't want my uncle to have the power to speak for me in any way."

"What are you babbling about?" Uncle Raymond demanded. "I'm making you my heir. What power do you want?"

"I want the kids in Buckley to be able to play soccer and baseball on the playing fields. I don't want condos built on that property."

Raymond slammed his fist down on the table. "You know nothing about this matter! With what nonsense is your lawyer filling your head?"

As I got to my feet, every bit of anxiety faded away. I felt clear-headed and in total control of what I was about to say. Four pairs of eyes focused on me, which only served to make me feel more confident.

"Chuck hasn't told me what to say. In fact, he doesn't know what I'm about to say."

"In which case, maybe we'd better discuss it first," Chuck advised.

"I don't think that's necessary." I fixed my gaze on my uncle. "Do you have a copy of the deed to the property in question?"

"Of course I do!"

"Interesting, because I've been told the one in Town Hall is missing."

Raymond threw up his hands. "That's not my concern! It's not my business to keep track of how official papers are filed in Town Hall."

"I believe it is," Chuck said calmly, "since you're the town council's official record keeper."

"True, but as you must know, there was a fire some years ago, and many records were destroyed. I'm-er-I'm busy trying to sort things out."

Sure you are. Aloud, I said, "I believe the property we're talking about belongs to all living Davenports."

Raymond's mouth fell open. He quickly recovered. "That's you and me, Simon. There's no one else remaining in our family."

I didn't know what to say. I was afraid to name Great-Aunt Lucinda. Raymond would want to know how I knew about her, then ask if I'd met her. I dreaded to think what he'd do if he learned Lucinda was my ally.

To my relief, Chuck said, "What about Lucinda Davenport? When last I heard, she was alive and well."

Raymond waved dismissively. "My aunt's nuttier than a fruit cake. She won't care what I decide to do with the property."

"How do you know?" I asked.

My uncle shrugged. "I'll ask her tomorrow."

Would Lucinda stand up to him? I felt my advantage slipping away.

"But I don't want you to build condos on the playing fields!"

My uncle shot me a puzzled look. "Why, Simon? As my heir, you'll benefit from the new condos. It will bring new life and new money into the community."

"But I want the kids to have a place to play ball." I hated that I sounded like a whining kid.

Judge Potter shook his head. "Simon, I regret to have to be the one to tell you, but as a minor, you've no say in this decision."

"I don't?"

Chuck intervened. "May I see the deed? As Simon's lawyer, I'd like to examine the document."

"Of course," Paul Garrison said. He slid one of the batches of stapled pages over to Chuck.

I watched Uncle Raymond converse with the judge in whispers. His face was the color of cherry soda. Though the air conditioning blasted away, he kept on mopping perspiration from his forehead with his handkerchief. I became aware of the odor of rotting vegetables. I wondered if my uncle was about to have a heart attack.

Still, seeing Raymond so cozy with Judge Potter made me uneasy. I turned to Chuck, who was frowning as he tossed the deed onto the table.

"I'm sorry, Simon. According to this deed, only Davenports over the age of majority can determine what becomes of the property, though you and every other Davenport will receive a percentage of the money from the sale or development of said property – an unusual set of conditions."

"All legal and binding," Paul Garrison pointed out unnecessarily. He smiled at me. "How I interpret it, you'll receive one-third of the profits of the condominiums. A nice hefty sum of money to start you on your way."

And so I'd lost. And what did I expect? I was only a kid. I had no way of bucking my uncle when it came to business. I doubted that Great-Aunt Lucinda could, either.

Judge Potter turned to me. "I think we'd better settle the matter of guardianship today."

"Unless Simon would like to begin proceedings to declare himself an Emancipated Minor," Chuck said.

The judge's double chin dropped onto his chest. "That's a very radical suggestion, Mr. Bayard. I suppose you've learned about it in law school and would like the chance to try it in court." He pursed his lips. "But this is a real person before us, a boy who's recently lost his entire family and has had the good fortune to be rescued by a blood relative he hardly knew. Adjustments take time."

He turned to me. "Does your Uncle Raymond beat you?'

I shook his head.

"Abuse you in any way?"

I paused then shook my head again. I wasn't about to fill the judge in on Raymond's habit of killing young girls for their life force or tell about the infusions. He'd think I was nuts and send me off for a battery of psychological tests.

Chuck bent toward me to whisper in my ear. "If your uncle's mistreating you in any way I can have the court look into it. You'll get a temporary court-appointed guardian."

"Someone I know?" I asked.

"That would be best," Chuck said.

Lucinda! I quickly scotched that idea. I didn't want to think how Raymond would retaliate if he discovered she was helping me.

"Simon, I wish you'd reconsider and let me take care of you," Uncle Raymond said.

Take care of me! That would be a laugh if it weren't so diabolical. I remembered Lucinda telling me I had to stay and battle my uncle. That I was strong enough to win. And if I kept my eyes and ears open,

I was bound to learn more about my uncle's powers as well as his weaknesses.

Judge Potter leaned toward me. In a kind voice, he said, "We try to keep minors with blood relatives whenever possible. Unless you tell us something specific that you object to regarding your uncle, any Family Court judge would move to have you live with your Uncle Raymond and Aunt Mary."

I cleared my throat. "All right, but I don't want to be adopted." I forced myself to meet my uncle's eyes. "If that's okay with you, Uncle Raymond?"

My uncle smiled. Gloated, was more accurate. "I'd be delighted, Simon, and I'll continue to hope that you'll change your mind about the adoption. It would make your Aunt Mary a very happy woman."

I couldn't bear to look at him a moment longer. "Mr. Garrison. Is there anything else that needs to be done?"

"No, I believe we've covered everything your uncle wanted to present to you."

I turned to Chuck. "Can we leave?"

"Sure." Chuck made a point of shaking hands with the three older men, but he was glum as the elevator descended to the ground floor.

"Sorry I wasn't more help to you, Simon. I didn't expect Judge Potter to be here. He's one powerful man."

I fought back tears. "My uncle knows everyone important and gets what he wants. What's the point of fighting him?"

Chuck didn't answer until we got into his car. "Your uncle's determined to go ahead with the condos, regardless of how many people sign the petition. He thinks he can handle your Great-Aunt Lucinda. But if she's for leaving the playing fields as is, we can fight it."

I shrugged. "She's against it, but what does that matter? Uncle Raymond has everyone in his pocket."

"If you dislike him that much, why didn't you agree to go the Minor

Emancipation route?" Cuck asked. "Judge Potter's powerful, but the court is obligated to hear your side of the story. And I get the feeling there's plenty you haven't spilled."

I turned away from his shrewd gaze. "It's complicated."

Chuck switched on the ignition. "I understand. He's still a relative."

A homicidal relative I have to keep under surveillance so I'll know what he's planning. "I guess."

Chapter Twelve

My cell phone rang as I was walking into the house.

"Simon, it's me—Lucy."

"Lucy!" I felt like tossing the phone in the air and shouting with joy until reality sank in. "You shouldn't have called me. Aunt Grace will be furious if she finds out."

"I don't care! She went to the store, so we can talk. I memorized your number from the last time you called."

My pulse thumped against my temples. "She left you alone?"

"I stay alone lots of times. I know not to let anyone inside."

I drew a breath. "Where are you?"

"Aunt Grace says you're only a half hour's drive from us, but she won't take me to see you."

"She's right, Luce. It's dangerous here."

"Then you come and stay with us. I want to see you, Simon." Lucy began to whimper. "I'm forgetting how you look."

I forced a laugh. "I look the same. But I bet you've grown an inch."

"Two inches. Aunt Grace bought airplane tickets to England. She said we have to move there." Now Lucy was bawling. "I don't want to go away. I want you to come get me, Simon. And take me to live with you."

"I can't do that, Luce."

"Then come visit me. We're in Parrish."

83

"Parrish! That's not very far from here."

"It's our third move. Aunt Grace took a job in an office. She says we need the money."

"And what do you do all day?"

"I go to day camp. Then I come home and stay in this hot, old apartment, and do nothing until Aunt Grace comes home from work. I hate it!"

"Lucy, please don't cry."

"I won't stay here another minute! If you don't come see me, I'll run away. And you'll never find me again!"

I knew she was exaggerating, but the thought of losing Lucy now blew me away. "I'll visit you, Lucy."

"Great, Simon! Come tomorrow while Aunt Grace is at work. I'll pretend I'm too sick to go to camp. She'll let me stay home alone."

A flash of terror ripped through me, chilling my bones. What was I thinking? Someone might follow me and see Lucy and me together. I had no idea how many spies Raymond had working for him.

"Lucy, we have to be careful."

"I know. We've moved twice because Aunt Grace was sure someone saw us. Who's after us, Simon? Aunt Grace won't say."

"I'm not sure," I lied, "but I'll make certain I'm not followed when I come to Parrish."

"There's a little park a few blocks from our apartment. We could meet there."

"Do you know the address?"

"Of course," she said, and rattled it off.

"I'll check it out on Map Quest. And look up the bus schedule."

"Okay. Meet me in the park at twelve noon tomorrow."

Tomorrow? It was so soon. But why not? I'd beg off going to camp after Raymond left for work, then make up some excuse to Aunt Mary. Even if they found out I'd left Buckley, I'd be back before they could figure out where I'd been. Tomorrow was the best possible day.

"All right, Lucy. We'll meet tomorrow in the park near your apartment."

"In front of the statue of the three children. Oh, I almost forgot. My name's Emma now. Even Aunt Grace calls me Emma. Maybe you should, too."

* * *

After dinner, I waited until my uncle left the house before going online to check the bus schedule to Parrish. One left at ten forty-five. There was a return bus at three thirty. Perfect. I'd get to spend a few hours with Lucy and be back in Buckley by the end of my camp day. I went downstairs to set my plan in motion.

Aunt Mary sat on the den sofa, knitting. Not knitting, I noticed as I entered the darkened room. Her hands remained still on whatever she'd been knitting, and her eyes were cast down. A silly sitcom playing softly on the huge TV.

"Aunt Mary?" I stepped closer.

She looked up. Her eyes were red. She'd been crying.

"Are you all right?"

She tried to smile, but it turned into an awful grimace. "Don't worry about me, Simon."

I put my hand on her arm. It felt soft and saggy, like an old cushion. "Can I do anything for you, Aunt Mary?"

She looked into my eyes. Her sadness felt as deep as a bottomless lake. I had to close my mind or her unhappiness would swallow me up. "You're a kind boy, Simon. I wish I'd been a better aunt to you. And now it's too late."

Panic gripped me in a stranglehold. "What do you mean? Are you sick?"

"Sick of myself." She gave a little laugh. "I've made a terrible mess of my life."

She was referring to her life with Raymond, but there was nothing I could say. I remembered why I'd come to talk to her. Time to move ahead with my plan.

"Aunt Mary, I'm not feeling well. I'm going to call Craig and tell him I won't be going to camp tomorrow."

"Of course, Simon. Do what you think best." She patted my hand. "It's been wonderful having you with us. You're the closest I've had to a son."

I bent to kiss her cheek, the first time ever, then took the stairs, two at a time, to make my call. I'd reached the top of the landing when it hit me that Aunt Mary hadn't asked about any of my symptoms. That and her words of regret made me hopeful that she'd come over to my side.

I told myself not to get too excited. Even if Aunt Mary no longer approved of my uncle's activities, she'd obeyed him for many years. Despite her good intentions, she was still under his control. I couldn't count on her help.

Craig wasn't home so I left a message on his tape saying tomorrow I wouldn't be coming to camp. I stretched out on my bed and made a mental list of what I had to do the following morning before getting on the bus: withdraw money from the bank and buy Lucy a small gift. I practiced the exercises Lucinda had taught me, then allowed myself to think about meeting Lucy. I placed my desk chair under the door handle and went to sleep early.

I awoke at six, my latest dream vivid in my mind. My parents, Lucy, and I were on vacation in the mountains. We were carefree and happy. I brushed aside my tears and leaped out of bed. I had to look ahead, to the time when Lucy and I could be together, far away from Raymond's evil influence.

* * *

At nine o'clock, I went into the laundry room where Aunt Mary was folding clothes and told her I was feeling better. "I think I'll go to camp today, after all."

Aunt Mary smiled. Her sadness had lifted and she was in better spirits. "Why don't you stay home today? I bet you could use a day off." She winked, surprising me. "It will be our little secret."

"Well," I began, suddenly feeling guilty about lying to her.

"Go on," Aunt Mary urged. "Spend the day in town, if you like. Or at the movies. I won't mention a word to Raymond."

This would be easier than pretending I was going to camp. "All right, Aunt Mary. In that case, I'll take off now. I should be home my usual time."

I grabbed my knapsack and kissed her cheek as if I'd been doing it since the day I moved to Buckley.

At the bank, I set up a pin number and withdrew one hundred dollars. Then I went to the general store-pharmacy to buy Lucy a present. I couldn't decide between a book and a pair of pretty barrettes, so I bought both. I left the store and checked my watch. It was ten o'clock. I had just enough time to walk to the bus stop half a mile away and buy my round trip ticket.

A car honked. I froze. One of my uncle's spies was tailing me! The car honked again. I walked over to the curb where it was idling and peered through the window. Inside in the driver's seat was Tasha Wells, the girl who had loaned me a pen in the library.

"Morning, Simon." She flashed me a smile as perfect as any smile in a toothpaste ad. "Where are you off to?"

"The bus station," I said, "and I'm running late."

"Hop in. I'll drive you there."

"You will?" As soon as the words left my mouth, I wished I could take them back. She'd just said she would drive me. "Gee, thanks."

She started down the block while I was closing the door.

"Hey! I'm not in that big of a rush."

Tasha laughed merrily. "Sorry. I'm hyper. Always two steps ahead of everyone else."

She drove fast, handling the car like a racing driver. "Where are you off to?"

What should I say? "I'm going to visit my sister," I answered, as though visiting my sister were an everyday occurrence.

"Ah," was Tasha's response. "Is she in camp?"

"Uh-huh."

At a red light, she turned to look at me. "I'm on my way to work." She giggled. "I'm fifteen minutes late, but the boss won't mind too much. He's my dad."

My dad. I'd have given anything to be able to say those words. To return to the time when seeing my father every day was something I took for granted.

Minutes later Tasha braked in front of the bus station. "We've arrived at your destination."

I thanked her and climbed out of the car.

"Stop by Carlie's, when you feel like hanging out. I'm there most evenings after nine."

I grinned, pleased by her invitation. The cheerleaders and jocks hung out in the ice cream shop. "Sure, I'll stop by."

"Do that." She took off.

My heart was racing when I entered the bus office to buy a round-trip ticket. Tasha Wells had invited me to hang out with her! The woman behind the counter handed me my ticket and my change and said my bus was boarding. I dashed off, all thoughts of Tasha Wells fleeing my mind.

I arrived in Parrish twenty minutes before noon. I was tempted to look for the apartment house where Lucy lived with Aunt Grace, but decided not to, in case someone had followed me.

Like Tasha? Maybe Raymond sent Tasha Wells to spy on me. I laughed at my paranoid thoughts.

Lucy was waiting for me in the park by the statue of the three children. We ran toward each other. I swung her around in my arms. She was much heavier than I remembered. After I set her on the ground, we grabbed each other in a fierce hug.

"Oh, Simon," was all Lucy could say. She sobbed noisily into the crook of my neck.

I pretended to be annoyed. "Hey, you're soaking my shirt."

"Sorry," she croaked.

We sat down on a bench and I studied her. "You've grown some."

"Of course I grew. I'm older, aren't I?"

The words cut me. We'd been apart for months, time I'd never get back. "And your hair's so short! It's darker, too."

"Aunt Grace colored it a few times," Lucy explained. "So maybe people won't recognize me." She searched my face. "What people, Simon? Who are we running from? Aunt Grace won't tell me."

I took a deep breath. "Our Uncle Raymond's a bad man, Lucy. Aunt Grace is protecting you from him."

Lucy wriggled her shoulders, something she did when she couldn't see the logic of her elders' explanations. "If he's so bad, why do you live with him?"

"I have to, for the time being. I've no choice."

Lucy studied me solemnly. Besides growing taller, I noticed, she'd shed a few pounds of baby fat.

"Does he beat you?"

"No."

Her face scrunched up in dismay.

"Does he force you to do things that are weird?"

I smiled at her concern. "Don't worry, Luce, he doesn't do anything bad to me," I lied. "But he does bad things to other children." I winced as I remembered Melissa Gordon. "To young girls your age." At her look of horror, I added, "Not what you're thinking, but bad."

I was relieved when Lucy didn't press me for details. But she had to understand the danger we were in and not do anything foolish. "I'm afraid he'd hurt you if he found out where you lived."

Lucy shivered. She put her hand in mine. "Will you take me out for lunch?"

We walked the few blocks to the nearby mall. As we passed stores, Lucy's eyes darted everywhere, grabbing in the sights.

"This is a great place!" she exclaimed.

"Haven't you been here before?" I asked.

She shook her head vehemently. "I told you, I stay home when I'm not in school or camp. Aunt Grace thinks it's safer."

She squeezed my hand. "I'm so glad you came today. I don't know what I would have done if you didn't."

I squeezed hers back and smiled. "I'm glad I came, too," I said, but my mood had turned black. I wondered if I'd done a terrible thing by coming today. Had I put Lucy's life in danger? I decided not to give Lucy the gifts I'd bought for her. If our aunt saw them, she'd go ballistic.

"Lucy, promise me you won't tell Aunt Grace that I came to visit."

Her hand crossed her heart. "I swear I won't." She lowered her voice. "And call me Emma."

"Emma," I echoed, the name as unfamiliar to me as the town we were in.

We took the escalator up to the food court on the second level. I sat Lucy down at a table. "What do you want to eat, Luce—Italian, Chinese, or deli?"

Lucy pointed to the corner kiosk. "They sell southern fried chicken there. I want two pieces and a soda."

"Two pieces of chicken and a soda coming up."

As I waited for our orders, I kept an eye on Lucy, ready to vault over to her at the first sign of trouble. But nothing happened. I put a broad smile on my face as I carried our food to the table.

"I'm starving!" Lucy exclaimed. She took her plate and soda from my tray. "You forgot the ketchup."

Before I could offer to get it, she jumped out of her seat and went over to the service area. I was about to take off after her, when she started back to the table.

"Don't ever do that again!"

"I only went to get—"

"I don't care! When you're with me, don't ever leave my sight."

Lucy burst into tears. "Don't be angry, Simon. I don't want you angry at me."

"Oh, Luce." I wrapped my arms around her. "I didn't mean to yell. I'm frightened because I worry about you."

"Why? Uncle Raymond isn't around." Her eyes filled with terror. "Do you think he followed you here? I don't want to die."

"You're not going to die." I had to move, leave the food court. I slipped on my knapsack and put our lunches back on the cardboard tray. "Let's go back to the park, Lucy. We'll have a picnic and talk about this some more, if you like."

"All right." She tucked her hand in my elbow, and we walked back to the park not saying much. I found a grassy spot besides some trees and within view of the children's playground. "Let's sit here and eat our picnic."

Lucy nodded. She'd stopped crying. Instead of the stream of questions I'd expected, she hunched her shoulders and stared down at the ground. Seeing her like this upset me more than her tears. Where was my spunky little sister, the kid who thought Gretel was the greatest for saving Hansel and herself from the witch? I wanted my old Lucy back.

I finished eating and asked Lucy if she wanted to talk about things.

"When will this be over and we can be together again?"

"I don't know, Luce. It will take time. Don't you like Aunt Grace?"

"She's all right. I want to live with you."

"That's what I want, too."

We walked around the park. The kids in the playground looked like they were having a great time. Like they hadn't a worry in the world. When I glanced down at my watch, I was surprised it was almost time to head for the bus stop.

"Let's walk to the statue where you waited for me."

"You're leaving," Lucy said, her voice breaking. "I don't want you to leave."

"Come on, Luce. You know I can't stay here. He'll send his men to look for me. I don't want them to find you."

"Our uncle?"

"Raymond."

"But he's our *uncle*. Why would he?"

"Because he's evil."

Her voice quavered. "What if he wins?"

"He won't," I said more firmly than I felt. "I'll take care of things, and then we can be together."

Lucy squeezed my hand. "Can I call you?"

"I don't think that's a good idea."

"Aunt Grace says we're going to England next week. I wish I could call you before we go away."

At the statue, I hugged her tight. "All right. Call me Saturday at one in the afternoon, or as close to one as you can. You know my number."

She buried her face against my chest and nodded. I hated to let her go. For a moment I considered staying, but I knew Raymond would send out his goons to find me.

I drew back and put my hands on my sister's shoulders. "You'll go straight home from here."

"Of course."

"I love you, Lucy."

"Emma," she whispered.

"No, Lucy," I whispered back. "Soon we'll be together again, and we'll never live apart until you get married."

Lucy giggled. "Or you get married."

I kissed her cheek and let her go. I jogged to the corner. At the red light I turned. In the distance, Lucy had stopped, too, and was waving at me. I watched her walk toward the apartment she shared with Aunt Grace.

Tears filled my eyes, and I brushed them away. Would we ever be together again?

Chapter Thirteen

I fell asleep on the ride home, and awoke with a start as we drove into Buckley. Where was I? Panic overcame me, until I realized I was on a bus, coming back from seeing Lucy. I glanced around at the other passengers. Had my uncle sent any of them to follow me? But none of them – not the heavy woman with two paper bags on the seat beside her, the scrawny old man dozing against the window, nor the young mother and her two children— struck me as likely spies.

Spending time with my little sister had been a precious gift. I wondered if I'd ever see her again. Aunt Grace was taking her to England next week. I shuddered. England was an ocean away. Despite all the positive things I'd said to Lucy, there was a better chance our evil uncle would win. Me, Simon Porte, would exist in name only.

A wave of desolation swept over me, nearly bringing me to tears. I'd give it a good fight, but I was only a kid – not yet sixteen. Yesterday at the lawyer's office had showed me just how powerless and naive I was.

When I arrived home, I tossed my knapsack on the hall floor and called out, "Aunt Mary, I'm home."

She descended the staircase, a finger to her lips. "Shh, Simon. Your uncle is sleeping."

"Sleeping? It's four-thirty in the afternoon."

"I know, dear, but he's not well. Raymond's had one of his turns."

Great news! Maybe he'll die and this horror will end.

I followed Aunt Mary into the den and sat beside her on the sofa. I remembered Raymond's high color in the lawyer's office, the perspiration on his forehead. I took her hand and asked, "Is it his heart?"

She nodded, blinking back tears. "His secretary drove him home after his business lunch. She wanted to take him to the hospital, but Raymond insisted he'd be all right after he got some rest. I called his doctor. He's coming by to see him after office hours."

She took a jagged breath. "Raymond's been working too hard these past few months, especially lately, with this condo deal in the wings." She squeezed my hand. "I told him he was overdoing things, but he laughed and said he was stronger than ever. His heart condition was a thing of the past."

"Maybe it's only a temporary setback," I said to calm her. I pressed my elbows against my sides to stop the trembling. The only way my uncle's health would improve would be through the death of another child.

Aunt Mary patted my cheek. "You're a good boy, Simon. I'm thankful you came to live with us." She tried to smile. "Did you have a nice day?"

"Very nice."

"I'm glad." Her hands flew to her face in dismay. "But with all this turmoil, I never got to make you dinner. Why don't you call the local pizza parlor and order a pie for yourself?"

"What about you?".

"I'm too upset to eat more than tea and toast."

I called in an order for a small pepperoni pizza, which was delivered some twenty minutes later. While I was downing my third slice, the doctor arrived. He conferred with Aunt Mary, their heads bent toward one another, then he followed her upstairs. He came down shortly after, talking to Aunt Mary over his shoulder. He reassured her that Raymond's heart was no worse. But he was overdoing it and needed two or three days of bed rest and shouldn't go back to the office until the following week.

After the doctor left, I sat down at my computer and googled airline sites to check out flights to London. Wow! I didn't expect it to cost that much. Prices were lower in September, but I couldn't wait that long. I was about to look into sites that offered cheaper rates, when the doorbell rang. I listened at my closed door and heard Aunt Mary greeting Craig Averil.

A minute later Craig was bounding up the stairs to the master bedroom and closing the door behind him. I waited a few minutes before leaving my room. The sound of the den TV downstairs assured me that Aunt Mary was occupied. I crept along the hall to my aunt and uncle's bedroom, and put an ear to the door. My uncle and Craig were chuckling, clearly pleased with themselves.

"I can relax like the doctor ordered," Raymond said, "now that you've taken care of our little problem."

The short hairs on my neck rose like soldiers. What evil act had Craig performed for my uncle?

"It was easy as pie," Craig boasted. "I knocked on her door and called out, saying I wanted to talk about the playing fields land. She assumed I was on her side and invited me inside. I used a rock I'd picked up on her front lawn. One blow and she went down for the count."

I gasped. Too late, I clamped my hand over my mouth, terrified they'd heard. They must not have because their coldblooded conversation continued.

"The question remains, how do you know she'll stay down? Lucinda's old, but she's one tough cookie."

"I felt her pulse," Craig said. "It's weak and she's unconscious. Who's going to wake her up? And if she comes to, who will hear her calls for help?"

Lucinda! Averil had struck Lucinda and left her for dead! I longed to rush inside the bedroom and knock him to the floor, then put my hands around my uncle's neck and squeeze until all life was gone. But I had to get to my aunt. She couldn't die!

My uncle's voice dropped to a whisper. "Don't forget the other little matter. That's even more important, if everything's going to work."

"I'll take care of it later tonight."

Four, eight, six, one. Four, eight, six, one. I repeated the numbers in my head as I flew down the stairs. *Wake up, Lucinda. Wake up!*

I stopped at the den where Aunt Mary was knitting and watching television. From her dull, confused expression, I figured she'd taken a sedative.

"Aunt Mary, I'm going out for a while."

"Okay, Simon. Don't come back late."

I repeated the four numbers again and again like a mantra as I raced to Lucinda's house. Silence. It was like phoning someone who wasn't home. As I approached Willow Road I sensed a presence. As though someone was coming to life—or consciousness.

"What?"

Her voice came through, weak and querulous, sending a burst of energy through my body. I forged ahead, my legs pumping harder and faster. "It's me, Lucinda. Are you all right?"

"Of course not! I'm dying."

"You're not dying! You can't!" My pulse clanged against my temples. My heart beat so fast, I thought it would burst. *No more deaths! No more deaths!*

Her breath sounded raspy. "Help me, Simon."

"I'm almost there. Try to sit up."

Lucinda moaned. "My head hurts."

The front door was ajar. I found Lucinda on the sitting room floor, half propped up against the sofa. She reached out a trembling hand.

"I'm here." I sank down beside her and felt the pulse in her wrist.

Weak but steady.

"You're a good boy, Simon." Lucinda blinked. "How did you know I needed you?"

"I overheard Craig Averil tell Raymond at the house. He struck you down and left you for dead."

She frowned. "Craig did?"

I gaped at her. "Don't you remember?"

Lucinda blinked as she tried to remember. "I was drying my dinner dishes then I don't know what happened – until you woke me up, my head aching something awful."

"Ohmigod!" How could I have forgotten to call for help? I patted my pocket. No phone. "Be right back!" I ran into the kitchen and dialed 911.

"I just got to my aunt's house and found her unconscious. Lucinda Davenport. She lives at 21 Willow Road. Send an ambulance immediately!"

The dispatcher told me help was on the way. Then I called Aunt Mary to say I'd be staying overnight at Andy's.

"All right," she said, sounding half asleep.

The Coltranes' house was the best place for me to stay if I managed to thwart Craig's plans and come out alive

Lucinda appeared to be sleeping. I shook her shoulder until her eyes fluttered open.

"Wake up! I've called for an ambulance. It will be here soon."

She winced. "And go to the ER? I hate hospitals. They're full of infections."

"Maybe so, but you might have a concussion."

"I suppose the sensible thing would be to get myself checked out," Lucinda said. She squinted, as though she were having trouble following her thoughts. "Why would Craig Averil want to hurt me? He's such a nice young man. Of course, I haven't seen him in years."

I let loose a raspberry. "He's a creep. He does Raymond's dirty work."

My aunt surprised me by clucking her tongue. "Poor Craig. I suppose he sold his soul to the devil because of his son."

"What are you talking about? I didn't know Craig has a son."

Before Lucinda could answer, a siren sounded, growing louder and louder almost muffling the ringing of the doorbell. I ran to open the door for the EMS.

Chapter Fourteen

A t first the EMS people said because I was a minor I couldn't ride in the ambulance with Lucinda. She carried on, shouting she wouldn't go to the hospital without her nephew. Finally, the head EMS guy—a really fat dude—gave in and told me to get in the back of the ambulance with her. I obeyed, and looked down so he wouldn't see I was grinning. My life was a total disaster, but I had one adult relative who gave a damn about me.

When we got to the hospital, I followed Lucinda's gurney into the ER. I helped her with the paper work, then held her hand while we waited in an examination cubicle.

A very efficient nurse came in and swung the curtains shut. She took Lucinda's blood pressure then turned to me. "The doctor will examine your aunt after she has a CAT scan. You can wait for her in the waiting room."

I sat there, skimming through practically every magazine, until a young Indian doctor came looking for me.

"We'll be keeping Miss Davenport overnight and possibly another day or two to watch over her condition," he said.

"Will she be okay?" I asked. "She told me she thought she was dying."

Dr. Mehta smiled. "I don't think she's about to expire. She's suffered a concussion, but her heart and other vitals are strong."

"Thanks. That's good to know."

The doctor lowered his voice. "Your aunt appears to have been struck by a blunt instrument. Were you present? Did you see what happened?"

I shook his head. "I was coming over to visit Aunt Lucinda. She was barely conscious when I got to her house. I called 911."

"We have to report all signs of violence to the police. An officer will be here shortly. Would you mind answering a few questions tonight? Or you could go down to the station tomorrow if you'd prefer."

"I'll talk to someone now," I said, hoping Dr. Mehta couldn't hear my heart popping like a ping pong ball against my ribs. I could just see myself explaining to the officer the truth about Lucinda's injury:

"What happened is my uncle, a member of Buckley's town council, ordered his friend, a popular high school teacher who runs a local day camp, to assault his elderly aunt because she stands in his way of a great business venture."

Right. That was sure to go over big with the police, who Raymond probably had in his pocket.

Dr. Mehta had me wait in a tiny cubicle of an office. Was it legal for a cop to question me without the presence of an adult? I started to worry, then realized Raymond wasn't well enough to leave his bed. It would have to be Aunt Mary, which might not be too bad.

Finally, a burly cop entered the small cubicle. He closed the door, then sat down behind the desk.

"Well, young man. It sounds like you've had one hell of an evening."

"I guess." Something I'd seen in a movie or on TV—or maybe knowledge Raymond had passed on during one of his infusions – warned me not to offer any information.

The cop seemed to sense this. He let out a deep sigh.

"Okay. I'm Sargent Baker of the Buckley Police. I'd like you to state your name and address, and tell me what transpired when you entered your aunt's house."

I decided to stick to the truth as far as I could. I said I'd come to visit Great-aunt Lucinda, which I occasionally did in the evening, and found her on the floor fading in and out of consciousness. "I called for help and the ambulance brought us here."

"You didn't see who struck your aunt?"

"No."

"See anyone running from the house?"

I paused. Now would be a good time to implicate Craig. But Raymond would probably give him an alibi.

"I didn't see anyone," I finally said.

"You're certain?"

"Yes."

Sergeant Baker shrugged, but his keen eyes never stopped scrutinizing me. It was like being x-rayed. "You didn't, by chance, happen to get into an argument with your aunt? Pushed her so she fell and hit her head?"

"Of course not!" I jumped out of my chair, knocking it over. "I love my Aunt Lucinda! And if you're going to start accusing me instead of going after the guy who did this, you're wasting everyone's time!"

He moved a finger up and down. "Cool it, Simon, and sit. I had to ask."

I did as I was told.

"I talked to Lucinda. She can't remember who attacked her. That happens lots of times with head injuries. But she nearly blew a gasket when I suggested maybe you did it." He grinned. "She insists you saved her life."

I shrugged. I'd gotten through, so far, but it wasn't over.

"I don't for a minute believe you struck your aunt, then accompanied her to the hospital." Sergeant Baker smiled. "Much less agreed to hang around here to talk to the police."

"Will Aunt Lucinda get police protection when she leaves the hospital? I don't want someone taking another potshot at her."

"I can't promise, but there's a good chance she will. The Davenport family has deep roots in Buckley."

"Good to know." I hightailed it to the door when he called my name. I spun around, surprised to find myself staring into Sergeant Baker's face. How did a man that large move so quickly and silently?

He handed me a card. "I get the feeling you know more about this than you're willing to say. Any time you want to talk, I'm willing to listen."

I looked down at the list of numbers. "Sure." I turned again, ready to flee.

"One more thing. I understand you came here by ambulance. How were you planning on getting home?"

"Taxi, I guess."

"Why don't you look in on Lucinda while I find a nurse who's coming off a shift and can give you a lift home?"

I smiled. "Thanks, Sergeant Baker. I'd appreciate that."

"Any time, Simon. Keep in touch."

I found Aunt Lucinda dozing peacefully. I kissed her cheek. Fifteen minutes later, I was in a battered pickup truck belonging to a strapping black orderly named Topper Harding and halfway to Craig's house. I'd told him I was spending the night with a friend. Topper was too busy describing the new smart phone he'd bought to ask any questions. I made the appropriate grunts of approval to show interest in the many advantages of his new phone, while I silently prayed I wasn't too late to save a young girl's life. Craig was bigger, older, and brawnier than me, but I had to do what I could to prevent another killing.

Topper turned onto Edison Street, where Craig lived. "That's the house." I pointed to a house that had lights shining from a window.

"Here you go then," Topper said as he swung into the driveway.

I hopped out and waved Topper on.

"I'll wait till someone lets you in," he said.

"No need," I said. "Really. Thanks for the lift." I prayed he'd back out of the driveway before someone came out, demanding to know what we wanted.

Topper grinned. "Sure thing. Stop by and see me when you come visit your aunt."

I watched him drive away. Then I pulled out the slip of paper where I'd written Craig's address. I figured he was halfway down the block.

Craig's SUV straddled the two-car driveway. I breathed a sigh of relief. He hadn't left yet for his evil mission. He couldn't possibly had had enough time to find a young girl and bring her to my uncle. I cringed as Raymond's memory of a young girl with an awful plastic tube emerging from her mouth flit across my mind. So this was how my uncle drained a child's life force and made it his own. I had no idea how Craig intended to get the girl past Aunt Mary. Then I remembered her confused expression when I'd left the house. Either my aunt had taken a sedative or Raymond had done something to dull her senses. She'd sounded awfully groggy when I called to say I'd be staying overnight at Andy's. She'd be sound asleep by now.

It suddenly occurred to me that Craig had told my uncle that he'd be taking care of the matter later. Where on earth would he find a nine-year-old girl hanging around town close to midnight? Or did he break into homes?

A light shone through the gauzy curtains of a second story window. Craig was getting ready for what he probably considered his second killing of the night. I frowned, trying to wrap my brain around the fact that the man was a hired assassin *and* a teacher. I'd seen him in school and at the day camp, and I could tell that Craig really liked kids. But he also killed people. Kids. Kids he knew. How could he do it?

Lucinda had mentioned something about Craig's son, but then the EMS people arrived and she'd never got to tell me the whole story. I couldn't imagine what could have turned Craig into a monster as evil as Raymond.

And now he was coming downstairs. He'd be outside in half a minute. I froze, not sure what to do. Ambush him? Try to reason with him? Neither would work.

I pulled on the back door handle of the SUV. It was unlocked and opened easily. I was about to crawl inside when I realized I needed a weapon. A steel pipe lay across the floor. I lifted it, felt its heft. Maybe this was what Craig used to knock his victims unconscious. No, that was the red silken cord coiled on the back seat.

The front door opened. I slid onto the floor of the back seat and closed the car door quietly. A minute later, Craig slid into the driver's seat. He turned around and, while I feared my thumping heart would give me away, reached for the silken cord and stretched it over the back of the passenger seat. Then Craig switched on the motor and music blasted through the vehicle, hurting my eardrums. It was an opera aria sung in German, I wasn't sure which though I'd heard it before. Craig lowered the volume and sang along as he backed out of the driveway and drove on his way.

Where were we headed? Craig maintained a steady speed of thirty, thirty-five miles an hour. He made several turns and stopped for a few lights, which meant we were still on local streets. We'd gone far enough to have passed the entrance to the Northway. Did Craig intend to choose his victim in Buckley? I shuddered to think Craig had access to the address of every nine-year-old girl who attended Shady Brook Day Camp. Was he planning to break into one of their homes? I gripped the metal pipe as I tried to anticipate Craig's plan.

Raucous music seeped into the SUV at the same time I caught sight of the houses. They were dilapidated with sagging porches, and close to one another. This was the old part of town. The poor part. From the floor of the SUV, I could make out the heads of people sitting on stoops, kids gathered on a corner, music escaping from boom boxes and open windows. It was past midnight, but here on this warm August evening, many residents were socializing outdoors.

The SUV slowed down to a crawl. Craig's head bobbed from left to right. *He's searching for a victim. God, don't let any little girl be outside all by herself.* Craig turned left. He shut off the AC and opened his window, letting in a blast of warm air. The street sounds grew louder. I heard girlish giggling.

Maybe he won't find a kid on her own. Who would allow a little girl to walk by herself in the middle of the night? Television laughter. A door slammed shut. Silence except for the pitter patter of a child skipping along.

Craig applied the brakes. We stopped.

"Excuse me, young miss. Where's twenty-five thirty-six Elm Street?"

The girl called from the sidewalk. "It's around the corner, Mister. Good-night."

"Could you just tell me – should I turn back or make a left at the corner? I've circled twice and I must have missed Elm. I have to pick someone up for the station, and he'll miss his train if I keep bypassing his house."

He sounded so kind, so concerned. I wanted to shout at the girl to run, run, as fast as she could.

The girl giggled. "You can't turn around. This is a One-Way Street."

"Oh. I didn't realize. How do I get to Elm Street?"

She moved closer to the car. "Go straight for two blocks. Then turn left. I'm not sure of the numbers."

"Okay. Will do." Craig's arm zipped out the window and grabbed her around the throat. The girl began to cough. Craig opened his door, still holding onto the girl through the open window. She made sputtering noises but nothing loud enough to draw attention. *Where was the kid's mother? Didn't anyone care about her?*

I sat up and peered out the window. Craig was in the street, the girl tucked under one arm. He held a hand over her mouth to keep her from screaming. She squirmed in his grip and pounded his back.

"Stop that, you little – "

Good girl! Keep on fighting! I yanked the key from the ignition and tossed it on the floor by the passenger's seat. I grabbed the metal pipe and stepped out of the car. Craig must have struck the girl hard enough to cow her into submission, because she hung over his shoulder like a sack of potatoes, whimpering softly.

"Let go of her!" I shouted.

Craig spun around to stare at me. "What the hell are you doing here?"

"Making sure you don't hurt anyone else tonight. Put her down. She's only a kid."

"Get out of my way!"

Craig strode around the front of the car and yanked open the passenger door. In a minute he'd toss the girl inside and drive off. It was now or never! I pulled back my arm and slammed the metal pipe down on his exposed shoulder.

The man was strong! He grunted from the pain and nearly dropped the girl, but recovered his balance and started pushing her inside. I whacked him again, this time on the side of his head. "That's for Lucinda," I snarled.

"Ow!" Craig crumpled to the ground. The girl slid from his grasp, as limp as a rag doll. I grabbed her in time to stop her from falling. She was thin and wiry, smaller than Lucy, and terrified with fear. "Run!" I shouted. "Run home where it's safe!"

She nodded but remained frozen as Craig stumbled to his feet.

"Go on!" I shoved her. She took off down the block.

Craig moved toward me, clenching and unclenching his fists. "Why, you interfering – "

I stepped back and picked up the pipe I'd let fall. "Keep away from me or this time I'll smash your head in two."

"You and who else?" Craig inched closer. "Wait till your uncle hears how you screwed up his plans."

Should I hit him again or make a run for it? Craig had four inches and at least thirty pounds on me. I'd only managed to get in those whacks because he'd been carrying the girl.

"There he is!"

"Get him!"

We both looked up at the three men running toward us. The girl must have told them what had happened. Craig pushed past me and jumped into the SUV. I sprinted off in the opposite direction. From the corner, I watched the men pounding on the car. The SUV came to life and sped away. Too bad. I should have thrown the keys out the window.

Chapter Fifteen

I fled, a primal instinct driving me far and away from that godawful scene. I ran until my chest hurt and my legs refused to take another step. I threw myself down on someone's lawn, ignoring the dampness seeping through my jeans. I remained sprawled on the ground, heaving and panting until my pulse returned to normal. I had no idea where I was. Not that it mattered. For the moment I was safe.

A train whistle sounded. I sat up and looked around to get my bearings. When I spotted the water tower, I knew I was on the other side of Buckley's downtown area. I got to my feet, ready to continue on. I was three miles from home.

Home? Hah, that was a good one. I had no home.

I started walking just to keep moving. I knew this neighborhood. I'd run through it many times. The homes were old and large, on plots three and four times larger than those of the homes where my aunt and uncle lived. Many of them had detached garages and sheds. I veered off the main road and followed a curving one-lane path to a manor house beyond a copse of trees. Its owners were either away or fast asleep because there were no visible lights.

I walked up the bluestone path to the front door, then around to the back. A pool glistened in the moonlight. I tried the door of the small cabana, and let out a sigh of relief when it opened. Phew! The place stank from chlorine and the odor of damp bathing suits, but I couldn't be particular. Clean towels were piled on one of the shelves. I spread a few on the floor and stretched out. Minutes later I was fast asleep.

I awoke achy and stiff the next morning. *Where was I?* I experienced a terrifying moment of panic. Then last night's events came crashing into my skull. I groaned, wishing I could trade the memory for the panic and not-knowing.

I had no idea what I was going to do next, except that I needed a change of plans. Saving two people's lives yesterday, was like putting a finger in the dike. Raymond was a monster. The devil. He'd sent Craig Averil out to do his dirty work, and sooner or later Craig would kill more people as he'd done in the past.

I gnawed at my lip. I'd made a big mistake not telling the cop that Craig Averil had attacked Lucinda. Then I remembered she hadn't actually seen Craig and might have said so to the cop. Though I'd witnessed Craig trying to abduct that little girl, it was my word against his. And even if they found the girl, they might not believe her. I shook my head in disgust. I had no hard proof to bring against a man with the reputation of being an excellent teacher and a law-abiding member of the community.

I had to leave Buckley! I had to convince Aunt Grace there was no way I could survive in this town. She had to take me with her and Lucy when they left the U. S.! If we needed money, I'd quit school and take whatever job I could find. Aunt Grace had to realize my life was over if I stayed here another day. I'd get Lucy to convince her. Lucy was only a kid, but she was smart and mature for her age. She was calling Saturday. Tomorrow.

I reached into my jeans' pocket. My cell phone was gone! I jammed my hand into my left-hand pocket. Empty. Frantically, I checked my back pockets.

Nothing.

Where was it? Had it fallen out when I was crawling around in the back of Craig's SUV? Had that creep found it? Could he trace Lucy's phone calls? My heart thudded against my ribs as I considered what would happen if Lucy called and Craig answered. Craig would trace the call and go after Lucy. And then –

I realized I was hyperventilating. I sank onto the bench of the cabana and forced myself to take cleansing breaths. I needed to be calm. To cool down and clear my mind. Otherwise I'd go off half-crazed and make mistakes. I couldn't afford another mistake. My sister's life depended on it.

I wanted to retrace my steps and chase down my cell phone. Or had I left it in my room, hidden among my things? *Think back!* Had I used it to call Lucinda?

Yes! *No.* I'd contacted her using the numbers she'd told me to memorize. I didn't have my phone at Lucinda's house, so I'd used her phone to call 911 and Aunt Mary . I release a huge sigh of relief. At least there was no chance that the phone was in Craig's SUV.

I pushed open the door of the cabana, checked to make sure no one was around, then stepped outside. It was a sunny August morning. As I walked toward the road, I heard the sound of a lawnmower. A dog barked. Cars sped by in both directions, carrying people to work, to school, or wherever they were headed. It was the start of another ordinary day for most people. For people who weren't related to Raymond Davenport, and weren't the devil's pawn.

I stood at the curb of the road and stretched out my muscles, then I started to run. I paced myself and jogged slowly toward the center of town. The large clock on the second story of the bank building said eight o'clock. Without making a conscious decision, I turned in the direction of my aunt and uncle's house. Only a few blocks to go.

As I ran past the last light on Main Street, I wondered if I'd dropped my phone on my way to Lucinda's house. Or had I left it in its hiding place? Maybe I'd be lucky, and the phone would be there. And if it was, then what? I almost laughed aloud. I'd have enough time to shower, change clothes, and catch the camp bus.

But why go to camp when I was about to make my big break? I had better things to do with my time like – I couldn't think of anything at the moment. It might be wise to behave as normal as possible and not tip off my uncle or Craig regarding my plans.

Craig would be furious at me for thwarting his plans last night. He'd probably want to kill me. But he wouldn't kill me. I smiled as it dawned on me that Craig wouldn't harm a hair of my head. Not as long as dear Uncle Raymond called the shots.

I doubted that Craig, tough as he was, had dared to risk another killing last night. Which meant—I found myself grinning—that my uncle must be pretty damn weak right now.

I opened the front door and breathed in the aroma of freshly brewed coffee. Though I didn't drink coffee, I loved the way it had made our house smell each morning when Lucy and I came downstairs for breakfast. Tears welled up as I suddenly remembered my parents rushing about before going to work; Lucy complaining she couldn't find her favorite shirt. I started for the stairs, eager to search for my cell phone, when Aunt Mary appeared in the hall.

"Simon! I'm so glad you're home!" She threw her arms around me. "Please don't ever do this again! You must tell me if you plan to stay out. I care about you, you know."

Didn't she remember I called? Of course not. She'd been drugged. "I called to tell you I was staying over at Andy's." I held my breath, hoping she hadn't called the Coltranes.

Puzzled, Aunt Mary put a hand to her cheek. "Did you? How could I have forgotten?"

I kissed her. "Probably because you were half asleep when I called. I'd better jump in the shower quickly if I'm to make the camp bus on time."

"I'll toast a muffin for you."

"Thanks, Aunt Mary."

She put her finger to her lips. "Try not to wake up your uncle. He's had a bad night."

I nodded. Waking Raymond was the last thing I wanted. I raced up the stairs, eager to know if I needed to start a wild hunt for my cell phone. I'd reached the landing and was turning toward my bedroom, when my uncle called to me.

"Simon, come in here. We need to talk."

I paused to think, and decided to ignore him. Raymond could scream all he wanted, but I wouldn't oblige him – not any longer.

"Please, Simon! Come into my bedroom."

Why? To get a lecture? By now he had to know I'd prevented Craig from kidnapping that little girl. Unless Craig had managed to kill another child after that. The thought made my stomach roil.

From deep within me, a voice of reason called me to task. *Do nothing rash. Find out he wants, then decide what to do.* Good advice. Regardless of how much I despised Raymond, I needed to know what he was thinking if I hoped to thwart his plans. If I was going to put an end to my uncle's vile activities, I had to anticipate his next move. And that meant hearing him out now.

The drawn shades kept the room in near darkness. The smell of rotting vegetables was back. I shivered. My uncle noticed and gave a snort of laughter.

"You can see I'm dying."

"Maybe that's a good thing."

"Not for me, it isn't!"

"It's good for other people. With you gone, Craig won't kidnap children for you to kill."

Another snort of a laugh. "He hasn't been very successful with you around."

I didn't answer.

"You're a smart boy, Simon. You managed to learn about life force transference from the only person who could have told you: Lucinda."

"Hurt her again and you'll die!" I stepped closer to the bed. My hands itched to press a pillow over my uncle's face. Raymond must have known what I was thinking because he shook his head.

"You won't do it. You're for life! Which is why I value you so much." Raymond laughed, genuinely this time, only it turned into a cough. "Besides, you can't stop the killing. It goes on, you know. Through the ages. For all time."

"You're evil," I said.

"Maybe so, but even I know when enough is enough."

I blinked, wondering if I'd heard correctly. "You're going to stop your henchman from any more killing?"

"That's right."

He's lying. A monster like Raymond doesn't give up this easily. "I don't believe you. You said yourself you don't want to die."

Raymond made a face. "The life force of other creatures can be transferred, though not as satisfactorily as a human's."

"Killing animals? That's cruel."

"That's life. Consider this: our animal shelters are overcrowded. They often euthanize a few dogs and cats in order to take care of the others."

Would the killing never end? A dark gloom pressed down on me, blocking out sunlight and all that was good in the world. I ran from the room, slamming the door behind me. It was like trying to quarantine someone with an awful disease, knowing the contagion would seep out anyway.

"I thought you'd be glad no one else is going to die ," Raymond shouted.

Glad? I stormed into my room. *Like I'm happy he'll be slaughtering*

114

innocent animals!

The cell phone was where I'd left it, in the deepest corner beneath my bed. I fished it out to see if anyone had tampered with it. Not that I could tell. I pulled clean clothes from my drawers and tossed them onto my bed. Then I took a fast shower. I had to move quickly if I was going to make the bus.

Chapter Sixteen

My cell phone rang as the bus turned onto the camp road. I pulled it from my pocket, hoping it wasn't Lucy after I'd instructed her not to call until Saturday.

"Hello, Simon? It's Chuck."

"Oh, hi." Flustered, I realized he was probably calling about his fee. "I know I should have paid you the other day. But you never told me how much – "

"There's no fee. Consider it my good deed for the week." Chuck's excitement came through. "You've more than earned it by helping our cause."

"What cause?"

"You know, the condos. I called your Aunt Lucinda and told her what the deed said about the Davenport property: it can't be sold unless seventy per cent of all family members who have reached their majority approve of the sale. Ms. Davenport's dead set against it!"

Lucinda? Lucinda's in the hospital. "When did you talk to her?"

"The other evening, after I drove you home. Why do you ask?"

I breathed a sigh of relief. "Just curious. Does my vote count?"

"That's what I've been looking into. Like most laws, it's complicated. Sixteen was the age of majority when the papers regarding the property were drawn up. Even if the court honors that age instead of eighteen, you don't turn sixteen until November. And we both know how keen

116

your uncle is to convert the playing fields into Condoland. We'd have to petition the court regarding the matter, given that you are in favor of keeping the land for its present use, and that you'll be sixteen in a matter of months. All of which might take some time." Chuck laughed meaningfully.

"Long enough so that if they honor sixteen as the age of majority, I'll be able to vote against the condos."

"Right. Unless your uncle pulls strings and gets a hearing on the calendar in September or October."

"When's the next town meeting scheduled?"

"September First, which is next Thursday night. The organizers figure everyone will be back from summer vacation by then. The more people in attendance, the more we can pressure Raymond Davenport to leave the playing fields as they are."

"Good luck with that. I have to go now," I said as the bus pulled to a stop and campers rushed past me to spill out the door.

To my surprise, it felt good being back in camp, giving kids swimming instructions and making sure they didn't clown around too much in the pool. I didn't mean to eavesdrop on a private conversation between a male and female counselor who were obviously in the early stages of their dating relationship, until the guy remarked that Craig wasn't at camp today. Hooray! One less complication to worry about – for the time being.

At lunch, I exchanged friendly banter with Andy and Pol. I was punchy from lack of sleep and yesterday's events. My nerves were as taut as the strings on a tennis racket. But instead of feeling irritable, everything the twins said struck me as funny. I laughed at the stupidest comment. I was leaving Buckley, once and for all. I had nothing to take care of until Lucy called. No more murders to worry about.

"Want to come over tonight?" Andy asked. "I downloaded a great new game and some new bands."

I was about to say I would, then had another idea. "Maybe. For a while." I cleared my throat. "Actually, I'm thinking of going to Carlie's around nine-thirty, ten."

"Carlie's?" Pol shot me a questioning glance. "That's where the jocks and cheerleaders hang out."

My face heated up. "Tasha said to come by some time. I told her I probably would."

Andy set down his hamburger to gape at me. "Are you talking about Tasha Wells? The cheer leader with the curvaceous bod?"

"What other Tasha do you know?" Pol asked. "And wherever did her parents find that ridiculous name?"

I squirmed, wigged out by the twins' reactions. Unflappable Andy was acting starstruck, like Tasha was a local Taylor Swift, and Pol was seriously annoyed. "Hey, you don't have to come with me."

"I want to go," Andy said. "How about you, Pol?'

"Wouldn't miss it," she said, her voice dripping with sarcasm.

I pointed at the blob of ketchup on Andy's shirt. "All right, but clean up your act and behave yourself."

Pol nodded. "That's right, Andy. You don't want to shame Simon in front of his new girlfriend."

"She's not my girl –" I began, but Polly had jumped out of her seat and was running toward the kitchen like she'd forgotten something important. She returned as I was tossing my sandwich wrapper into the trash. "I'll come by your house round seven-thirty tonight."

"See you then," Andy said.

Pol glared at me.

"Don't mind her," Andy said in a stage whisper. "Pol's in one of her snits."

"Really?" I had the feeling Pol was angry at me. "Why?"

Andy burst out laughing. "She doesn't need a reason. Just ignore her."

I found a quiet spot behind the building and silently repeated the necessary numbers to contact Lucinda. She responded after the third calling.

"Hello, Simon. Are you at camp?"

"Uh-huh. How are you feeling?"

"Better, though my head aches something dreadful."

"How long do you have to stay in the hospital?"

"I'm not sure. They want to do more tests. I can't rest. I may leave earlier than they planned."

"Don't! Let them do the tests, Lucinda."

Two male counselors walked by. They stopped talking to stare at me, probably wondering why I looked upset while I stared off into space. Philip, the taller one, reached out to put a hand on my shoulder.

"Hey, buddy, you okay?"

"Fine. I'm just working something out in my head."

Ron, the shorter counselor, blinked as he studied my face. "From your expression, it must be real heavy, dude."

"What's that?" Lucinda wanted to know.

I couldn't respond, not with the two guys scrutinizing me like they were waiting for me to do something bizarre.

"I hope whatever's bothering you works out all right in the end," Philip said.

"Me, too," I answered, relieved when they continued on their way.

"Simon, what's going on there?"

"Nothing, Lucinda. Some counselors came by and thought I looked upset and strange."

"Like you were daydreaming, I suppose." Lucinda chuckled. "They'd think it even stranger if they knew we were communicating without speaking."

I turned to face the building. "After I left the hospital last night, I stopped Craig from killing another girl."

"Oh, Simon! You're too young to have to fight your uncle and his ghouls!"

"Someone has to. Besides, Raymond said he'll stick to animals for now."

"Did he indeed?" She paused, then said softly, "I should have finished him off years ago when I had the chance."

I thought of my own lost opportunity, then blinked it away before Lucinda could pick up on it. "Raymond's sick, Lucinda. Maybe he'll die."

She sighed. "That would be a blessing." She yawned. "I'm dreadfully tired. I think I'll take a nap."

"Rest and get better. I need to talk to you about something. In private."

"Maybe I will stay here till Sunday like they want. We can talk Sunday afternoon when I'm home. Can it hold till then?"

"I guess." I stifled the urgency to tell her about Lucy now.

"Good. Meanwhile, go and enjoy yourself. A boy your age should have nothing on his mind but having a good time."

* * *

I whistled as I combed my hair, staring into the small mirror above my bureau. After showering, I'd put on a forest green rugby shirt with a white collar and clean chinos. I tied the laces of my sneakers, made sure my wallet and cell phone were in my pants pockets, then headed downstairs. I peered inside the den where my aunt and uncle were watching TV. It sounded like the local news.

"Good-night. I won't be back too late – around eleven-thirty, twelve."

"Have fun, dear," Aunt Mary said.

"Thanks, I will."

I strode toward the front door, when my uncle called out, "Where are you going and with whom?"

His tone seriously annoyed me. I considered not responding, but decided not to make waves. "I'm going over to the twins' house for a while, then we're going to Carlie's."

"Carlie's, eh?" Raymond asked, sounding pleased. "That's where the kids with status hang out. I wouldn't think the Coltrane kids traveled in those circles. Though I wouldn't be surprised if they brought you into the fold."

"You'd like that, wouldn't you?" I asked bitterly.

"You're darn tootin'."

My uncle's maniacal laughter echoed in my head all the way to the twins' house. I scowled as I followed his obvious train of thought to its logical conclusion. Raymond still counted on transforming himself into my body, and as me he liked the idea of being a member of the elite high school set. How pathetic! He had no idea I'd always been part of the so-called A Level group. I'd been one of my school's top track stars, a respectable left guard, and a damn good first baseman — none of which I now gave one hoot about.

I wondered what other atrocities Craig had performed to improve my uncle's health, enabling him to watch TV downstairs with Aunt Mary. Had he slaughtered a few cats and dogs? I shuddered, hating to think of their deaths. At least no little girls were being murdered.

As soon as I was living with Lucy and Aunt Grace, far from Buckley, I'd write down everything my uncle had done and send a copy to Sergeant Baker and another to Chuck Bayard. The police and the lawyers would have to prove the case against Raymond Davenport, and stop his evil once and for all.

Andy opened the front door, then flew back up the stairs expecting me to follow. I was glad to see he'd combed his hair and had put on a nice plaid shirt, though it stretched tight across his belly.

I'm becoming as big a snob as Raymond, worrying what Tasha will make of Andy's appearance if she shows up tonight.

Andy's new game was challenging. It had a New Age type of musical soundtrack I liked. We vied neck and neck to kill the most villains and reach the treasure of jewels. Engrossing as it was, I kept an eye on the clock. At ten to ten we'd each won a game apiece. We lounged back in our chairs, grinning at each other.

"Great game, isn't it?" Andy said. "Want to go another round?"

"I think we should leave soon."

Andy laughed. "I almost forgot. You want to go to Carlie's tonight."

"Uh-huh."

"You sure you want Pol and me tagging along? If you and Tasha have a date –"

"We don't have a date! And, yes, I'd like you guys to come with me. We'll have fun."

Andy shrugged. "All right with me. I hear they have a new coffee-ice cream drink that's dee-licious."

"Where's Pol?" I asked. Pol hadn't come in to talk to us once. In fact, I hadn't seen Pol all evening.

"In her room. Doing Pol things, I guess."

I suddenly felt nervous. "Isn't she coming with us tonight?"

"She said she was," Andy said. "I'll check."

"Thanks, 'cause I'd like to get going as soon as she's ready."

When Andy returned, he had a strange expression on his face. "Pol said to give her a few minutes. She'll meet us downstairs."

"What's wrong?"

"Nothing. Come on. We'll wait for her in the den."

A few minutes later, Pol poked her head inside the den. "All right. Let's go."

Andy continued what he was saying without looking at his sister. I stared at Pol. She wore jeans and a polo, but she looked different. Her hair was different. She'd pulled it back and piled it on top of her head.

For once she wore lipstick and eye make up. She looked – glamorous.

"Wow!" I said. "You look great."

"Thanks," Pol answered. "I don't want to embarrass you at Carlie's."

"You'd never embarrass —" I began, but she was halfway to the front door.

"Are you guys coming or what?"

* * *

Carlie's was mobbed with wall-to-wall teenagers. I doubted anyone inside was over twenty. I hovered in the doorway, the twins on either side, suddenly unsure of my next move.

"Let's find a table," Andy said. "Then I'm going to get the biggest coffee-ice cream drink they sell."

"If we can find a place to sit," Pol muttered as she looked around. "Maybe coming here wasn't such a great idea."

Her face was flushed, and I picked up on her discomfort. *Was Tasha here? Was dragging Andy and Pol to Carlie's one big, fat mistake?*

"There are a few empty tables in the back," Andy said, pushing his way through the crowd.

Polly and I followed. I'd crossed half the room when someone touched my shoulder.

"You came, after all!"

Startled, I gazed down at Tasha's smiling face, greeting me as if I'd just come in first place at a track event.

"I'm here with my friends, Andy and Pol Coltrane. Andy's gone to find us a table. This is Pol." I turned, wishing Pol wasn't scowling.

"Hi, Pol," Tasha said airily.

Pol gave her a half smile.

"We know each other from French class," Tasha said. "Come sit with us. We've plenty of room at our table."

I'll go get Andy," Pol said, and took off.

I felt self-conscious as I sat in the one available seat at Tasha's table. She introduced me to Jess, Tori, Ken, and Brian. When Pol and Andy appeared, Tasha told Brian to pull over two chairs. He did, but they didn't quite fit around the table.

The kids at the next table got up in one fell swoop, and Andy scraped back his chair to claim the table. "Pol, let's sit here."

I felt torn, wanting to sit with Tasha and her friends, but feeling I should be with the twins. I should have come alone. I'd only brought them along because I felt weird walking into Carlie's alone, wondering what I'd do if Tasha wasn't here or didn't want my company. But clearly she did because she was switching seats with her tall friend Jess, whom I remembered from the library, so she could sit next to me.

"What are you drinking?" she asked. Even with my keen sense of hearing, I had difficulty hearing her over the din.

"What's good?"

Tasha described a drink of a latte with vanilla fudge ice cream.

"Sounds good," I said. "I'll try it and buy you one."

When I passed Pol, she was sitting by herself. "Where's Andy?"

"He's getting our drinks."

"Great!" I said enthusiastically.

"Having fun?" Pol asked.

I turned, pretending I hadn't heard her over the noise. Pol was acting weird. I had every right to be annoyed with her. After all, she didn't *have* to come to Carlie's tonight. She could have stayed home. But somehow I felt it was my fault she was acting like this. And I should be sitting at the table with her and Andy. Only I'd come here tonight because of Tasha.

Back at the table, Tasha hung onto my arm and laughed a lot. We slurped our drinks and smiled at each other. We didn't say much – we couldn't because of the noise level – but I didn't care. A few juniors came in and joined Andy and Pol at their table. Jared Winston, a friend of the twins, sat down beside Pol. She seemed to liven up, which both relieved and irritated me. I had no time to wonder why Jared's arrival bothered me because Tasha was tugging at my hand.

"It's noisy in here. Want to go for a walk?"

I swallowed. "Sure."

Tonight was my lucky night! Tasha wanted to make out with me! Every cell in my body began to tingle. Where could we go for some privacy? Probably her car.

I got up and followed Tasha to the back door when Jess shouted out her name.

"What now?" She turned to her friend, who was frantically gesturing that she should return to their table.

Tasha shook her head. "I'll be back soon."

"You have to come now!" Jess called back. "Rick's here."

Tasha let out an exaggerated sigh as she retraced her steps, slowly as though she was returning to the table against her will. All for show, I knew, because her small frame gave off a raw wave of emotion that almost knocked me off my feet. She was fixated on the guy walking toward her. I'd been totally forgotten.

Rick looked to be a college sophomore, with the broad shoulders and confidence of a football quarterback. Though his face wore an expression of fury, I sensed his vulnerability and pain.

They stood inches apart scowling at each other. I hated how Tasha seemed to melt inside. How it took every bit of self-control not to throw herself into Rick's arms.

Though Rick spoke softly, I heard his words and his desperation. "Tasha, this is stupid. We need to talk."

Tasha turned away. Rick placed a hand on her arm as though it belonged there.

I pushed my way through the crowd. What an idiot I'd been to think Tasha was interested in me. Once again, I'd become somebody's pawn. A flash of anger shot through me. Tasha had used me like a boy toy—someone to flirt with and tease until she and her boyfriend made up.

I stood outside, ready to take off for home. What was I doing here, anyway, gushing over a flighty cheer leader? I had things to take care of, important things, like escaping from Raymond Davenport, and seeing to it he was put away so he could never kill again. I gulped down air, ready to take off, when I realized I had company.

"Ready to call it a night?' Andy asked.

I nodded.

"Pol and I will walk with you – unless you want to run home."

"I'd rather walk back with you guys."

We fell into step, a twin on each side of me. I gave Pol a half smile as we set off.

"Carlie's ice cream's not half bad," she said.

"Not half bad," I agreed.

I was glad Pol was no longer angry at me, and that she'd resisted making a nasty crack about Tasha. We walked home in silence, a comfortable silence that required no words.

As we approached the block where the twins lived, Andy asked, "what are you doing tomorrow?"

"I'm not sure."

"I'll probably go to the pool in the afternoon," Andy said. "It's supposed to be a scorcher."

"I'll probably go to the pool, too," Pol said.

"Oh, yeah? Then maybe I'll meet you there. Around two?"

"See you then," the twins said in unison.

I walked slowly the rest of the way home. Andy and Pol were friends. *Real* friends. They looked out for me and cared about me. I smiled, remembering how angry Pol had been earlier this evening. She knew

I was making a fool of myself with Tasha but hadn't the heart to spell it out. And Andy was always there for me.

I'd remember them long after I left Buckley.

Chapter Seventeen

The next morning I was helping Aunt Mary clear the breakfast dishes when the doorbell rang.

"I'll get it," Raymond called out. I gritted my teeth, hoping it wasn't Craig.

"Look who's come to visit!"

My mouth fell open as my uncle ushered Tasha into the kitchen. Raymond was beaming like a prospective father-in-law. The irony of the situation made me burst out laughing. Raymond thought Tasha had a thing for me, something he'd benefit from after the transformation. Well, my uncle was mistaken on both counts.

"Hi, Tasha. What are you doing here?"

"Simon!" Aunt Mary remonstrated. "Where are your manners?"

Tasha looked flustered. "I hope I didn't come too early and I'm not interrupting your breakfast," she said quickly, "but I need to talk to you, Simon."

"Okay. Talk."

Raymond made a sound of disapproval. "Sit down, my dear. Mary, is there any coffee left?"

"No, but I can brew some in a minute."

"Please don't bother! I'd like to speak to Simon. Privately." Tasha probably meant to smile, but it came out a grimace. She silently begged me to help her out. "Can we talk outside?"

"Sure." I unlocked the kitchen door. "Be right back," I said to Aunt Mary.

Tasha followed me outside. We started walking down the block without speaking.

"Simon."

"Yes?"

She managed to look apologetic and irritated at the same time. "Please don't make this more difficult than it is."

"I'm not doing anything. What did you want to tell me?"

"I'm sorry."

"For?"

Tasha gave a start. Clearly she'd expected her two-word apology to do the trick.

"For what? For leading me on. For throwing yourself at me until some guy named Rick came into the place and you forgot I even existed."

Tasha opened her mouth to argue, and closed it.

"I'm sorry for all that. I do like you. I mean, I think you're a great guy and everything – which you are – but I shouldn't have acted like that last night. Rick and I went through a terrible time last week. I thought it was over between us."

"Only it isn't."

Her face took on a dreamy expression. "No, we're together again. Like we should be."

I nodded. "I agree. You guys love one another and should be together."

She grinned and placed a friendly hand on my arm. "Thanks. I'm glad you see it that way."

I drew back, letting her hand fall. Her eyes widened in surprise. I had no idea where I'd suddenly gotten the nerve to tell her exactly how I felt, nor did I care. I charged ahead, giving it to her with both barrels.

"It doesn't excuse the way you came on to me." I met her gaze straight on. "You used me, Tasha."

She glanced away. "I wasn't sure Rick and I were getting back together."

"Sure you did."

"Maybe." Tasha had the grace to look ashamed. "I apologize."

"Apology accepted. Now if you'll excuse me, I'm going home."

"Wait!"

I stopped and waited 'till she caught up to me.

"I'm not used to guys reading me like a book they've read before. Telling me how to behave." She gave me this look of incredulity. "You're only a junior! How did you get so smart?"

I shrugged, not sure if she was flirting. I had no intention of getting caught up in her game.

"Hey, this time I'm not coming on to you. I like you, Simon. Enough to turn green with jealousy when I'll find out you're somebody's boy friend."

"Thanks – I think."

Tasha winked. "Maybe Pol Coltrane will be the lucky girl."

"Cut it out, Tasha. Pol and I are just friends."

Tasha tossed back her head and laughed.

"What's so funny?"

"For a smart guy, you're as blind as a bat. If those were real daggers she kept sending me last night, I'd be deader than a doornail."

My heart was racing. "Is that so?"

Tasha shrugged. "Find out for yourself."

We walked back to the house in silence. The weird thing was I was no longer angry. My feelings for Tasha had evaporated like they'd never existed. She'd been spoiled by having wealthy parents, good looks, and a charming personality. Even worse, she was devious, which I sure didn't need in a girlfriend. Still, I had to admire her spunk and energy.

We stopped at Tasha's car, which she'd parked in the driveway. She zapped the lock. "So, are we still friends?"

"Of course." I came around and opened the door for her.

Tasha slid gracefully into the leather seat. "See you around."

"Bye." I watched her drive away.

Raymond called out to me as I entered the house. "Where's Tasha?"

"Gone." I started up the stairs to my room.

"Did you make a date for tonight?"

I turned around to answer him. "Of course not. Tasha has a boy friend."

My uncle frowned. "Too bad. Maybe you can hook up with one of her friends."

I burst out laughing. "Hook up with one of her friends," I echoed. "Do you even know what that means?"

I locked my door and booted up my computer to check my email and last night's game scores. As I straightened up my room, I wondered how many more days I'd be living in this house. I grinned, remembering how disappointed Raymond had been to learn that Tasha and I weren't interested in each other. That was nothing compared to how he was going to feel after I disappeared from his life. The poor guy was going to have to live out the rest of his life in his old skin.

Eleven-thirty. Lucy wouldn't be calling for at least an hour and a half.

I tossed a swim suit and a towel into my tennis bag and went downstairs. Raymond was gone. Aunt Mary was straightening up the den. "Hey, Aunt Mary, I'm going into town for a bit. Then I'll meet the twins at the pool."

She looked up from dusting the TV, her hand to the small of her back. "It's a good afternoon for the pool. They expect the temperature to reach ninety-four. Would you like me to pack you a lunch?"

"No, thanks. I'll buy something at the pool."

"I'd keep away from hot dogs and hamburgers in this weather," Aunt Mary said. She covered her mouth, and quickly added, "Listen to me, rattling on about food when I'm sure you know what to eat."

I patted her back. "I do, but it's nice to hear it from you."

My words flustered her more. "Go on. Your friends must be waiting."

I grinned. "Let them wait." I reached down to hug her.

Aunt Mary squeezed me tight. "I've grown so fond of you these past few months."

"It's mutual."

She drew back to look at me. I got the definite impression she wanted to say more, but I couldn't read what was in her mind. All I picked up were her fear and confusion. Did Aunt Mary know what her husband had in store for me? Did she know he was evil through and through? She *had* to have some idea. Which meant—I couldn't bring myself to complete the thought.

"I'd better go."

"Have fun with your friends." She looked sad.

I walked slowly into town, mentally rehearsing what to tell Lucy when she called. I didn't want to frighten her, but she *had* to convince Aunt Grace that my life was in danger. I had to go to England with them.

I hoped there was an available seat for me on the flight to London. I had a passport because three years ago our family had gone on vacation in France. Where exactly was my passport? I exhaled loudly when I remembered having tossed it into a box of papers I'd taken with me when I moved out of the house six months ago.

When I got to the library, I checked out a sports magazine to have something to read while I waited for Lucy's call. I was about to exit the building when I spotted Pol scanning the bulletin board. I walked over to say hello.

"Hi, Simon. I just put up a notice about the playing field meeting –

the third one in as many days. Someone keeps taking it down."

"Oh." For a moment, I had no idea what she was talking about. Town meetings were the last thing on my mind.

Pol glanced down at my tennis bag. "Are you off to the pool?"

"In a while. You'll be there, won't you?"

Before she could answer, the four musical notes of my cell phone chimed. A passing librarian gave me a frosty smile. "We turn off our cell phones when we enter the library," she said.

"Sorry."

My phone sounded again. I glanced down. Lucy. "Hi. Just a second." I looked at Pol. "I have to take this. See you at the pool."

She scowled and turned back to the bulletin board.

She thinks I'm talking to Tasha. I'll explain later. I flew out the door and sat on the first empty bench.

"Hey, Luce, what's up? Are you okay?"

"No-o-o, I'm not."

Her sobs tore at me. A vise clamped around my heart, squeezing so I could hardly breathe. "What's wrong, Lucy? Did something bad happen?"

"I told Aunt Grace you came to see me and she got very angry."

"You shouldn't have done that, Luce. I told you not to say anything until we talked again."

"But I had to, Simon." Lucy hiccupped. A minute or two passed before she could speak. "I want you to come with us. I think we're flying to London on Tuesday."

"Tuesday," I repeated. *Three days from now! Nothing was going as planned.* "I have to talk to Aunt Grace! She has to help get me out of here! I'll call her and make her understand."

Lucy was sobbing again. "You can't! She doesn't want you to come with us. I begged her to take you, but she said her job is to make sure I'm safe and she can't do that if you're involved. She – she said she'll lock me up somewhere if I call you again. I said I wouldn't to get her off my back."

My head filled with rage. "She said she'll lock you up! What a wonderful, loving aunt she turned out to be!"

"Aunt Grace doesn't know beans about kids. She'll be home in a few minutes. Come and get me, Simon! We'll go someplace together."

Go someplace? Where could we go? Where would we be safe?

"Lucy, listen to me. This is important. You have to stay with Aunt Grace. She'll keep you safe. What I want you to do is give me the phone number at the apartment. I'll call and explain it's a matter of life and death that I go with you. Okay?"

I fumbled in my bag for the pen and paper I'd brought along.

"All right. It's —"

My sister's scream nearly pierced my eardrum.

"Lucy! Lucy!"

The line went dead.

Chapter Eighteen

hat to do? What to do? Frantically, I tried to reconnect to the number Lucy had called from and got what I expected: the number was blocked. I wanted to howl my anger and frustration. Lucy was in danger! Somehow, Raymond had gotten to her.

I ran over to the fence and kicked it with all my might, furious at the unfairness of it all. I had no home, no one to protect me. And now Lucy was in the clutches of that madman or one of his henchmen. I tried not to think of how frightened she must be. I had to find out where she was being taken. I had to save her. My poor sister. They'd caught her because I'd convinced her to meet me and call me. She was their prisoner now, and it was all because of me. I snatched up my tennis bag to do what I always did when things got impossible – I ran. Knees pumping, I hurled myself forward. I flew past the library and into the street, ignoring the sound of an angry horn as a car swerved to avoid knocking me down. The heat had thickened the air, making it difficult to breathe, but I ran. Ran faster. Sweat streamed down my face, my chest, my back.

When I came to Main Street, I was dizzy, heaving, and dying of thirst. As I slowed down, I reached for the bottle of water I always carried with me, gulping it down to the very last drop. Still lightheaded, I dropped into a chair outside of Starbucks and sat, head tucked between my knees until I caught my breath. I needed to figure out what to do. I needed a plan.

I had to talk to someone, and the only person who could begin to understand what I was going through was Great-Aunt Lucinda. I shook my head, defeated. The hospital was miles away. I'd have sunstroke if I continued to run in this heat.

Idiot! Stop panicking and use your brain. Call her before you move another step. I forced myself to sit calmly. I drew in deep, cleansing breaths. Silently I reeled off the numbers: 4-8-6-1. 4-8-6-1.

"Simon, is that you?" Lucinda's voice came through loud and clear. I smiled. She was on the way to recovery.

"Yes, Aunt Lucinda. I'm coming to talk to you, once I figure out the best way to get to the hospital."

She laughed. "I'm not at the hospital. They let me go home."

"Great."

Our connection broke down. I threw up my hands in disgust. What else could go wrong? A minute later, she was back. "Sorry about that. I now have an aide. She's in the kitchen. I asked her to heat up some soup before she leaves. I can't talk to you and to her at the same time."

"I thought they were keeping you in the hospital at least till tomorrow."

"I let them take a few of their tests. Then I carried on until they said I could go home if I arranged to hire a full-time nurse."

"You just said your aide's about to leave."

"Simon, don't start in on me!"

"But Aunt Lucinda – "

"My aide is my neighbor. Brenda's an R. N. We've agreed that she'll look in on me every few hours. Don't worry so."

"Can I come over now? I don't know what to do! I was talking to Lucy. She screamed suddenly, and the line went dead. I think Raymond sent someone to kidnap her." I thought a bit. "Or else Aunt Grace came upon her talking to me."

Lucinda tsk-tsked. "Simon, you mustn't interfere with your aunt's plans for Lucy."

"I have to! She's taking her to Europe in a few days. I'll never see my sister again!"

I must have been shouting, because people at neighboring tables were staring at me.

"Grace is doing all she can to keep Lucy safe. Try to be patient, Simon. In time you'll be with Lucy."

"Patient!" Oh no! I'd spoken aloud again. I swallowed, then forced myself to answer silently. "I can't bear to go on living like this! Raymond's a monster, but I can't tell anyone what he's done. Who would believe me? I'd end up in a mental hospital."

"We're going to tell the police what he's been doing."

"We are?"

Lucinda laughed, clearly delighted that she'd shocked me. "That's right. Come over now and I'll show you what I've found."

* * *

When we were sitting side by side on Lucinda's sitting room sofa, she held up a tiny round piece of metal with a hole in the center. "You see this?" she demanded.

"Uh-huh," I said. I hoped she hadn't lost her marbles.

"Now, I want you to go into the hall, get on your hands and knees, and search for a small pin with a piece of metal sticking out of it – like an earring on a post."

I stared at Aunt Lucinda. She *had* lost her marbles.

"Or a tic tack," she went on, ignoring my expression of disbelief. "Actually, it's a kind of a pin. I remember pulling on his jacket and hearing the pin fall on the tile."

I felt a surge of excitement. "You're talking about your assailant. Craig!"

Lucinda grinned, looking like a cat that had finished a bowl of cream. "If you say so. The pin will have his fingerprints on it, so when you find it, you'll have to scoop it up with a piece of cardboard so as not to get your fingerprints on it." She winked. "I saw that on TV."

I returned her grin. For the first time in days, in months, I felt optimistic. Finally, we'd have actual proof to support my story.

"I bet I know what you pulled off Craig's jacket. It's a camp pin. Every camper and counselor has one. We're supposed to wear it every day but no one does." I chuckled. "No one, but Craig, that is."

I dropped to my knees and examined every inch of the small hall. The pin was nowhere to be found.

"It's not here," I grumbled.

"Are you sure? I'll get you a magnifying glass. I have one somewhere in the house."

"I don't need a magnifying glass," I said as I crawled into the sitting room. "I've twenty-twenty vision. If it's here, I'll find it."

"Of course it's there. Did you check the closet?"

"No."

"Look inside the closet."

Lucinda's hall closet was dark and musty. Umbrellas, boots, and galoshes covered the floor.

"It's not here."

"Are you sure?"

"Of course I'm sure!" I peered up at my aunt hovering over me. "Sit down. I'll tell you when I find it."

"I just want to help," she complained, but did as I'd ordered.

I found the pin under a small end table at the entrance to the sitting room, where it must have rolled. "I see it! At least, I think it's the pin."

"Don't touch it! Don't touch it!"

"Why do you think I'm moving the table?" I asked, irritated. I scooped up the pin with the piece of cardboard she'd given me. "I need a small plastic bag."

"Coming right up!" Lucinda answered.

I followed her into the kitchen and placed the pin in the bag. "See," I said, " you can make out the words through the plastic: Shady Hill Day Camp. Craig must have dozens of these. I wonder if he knows he left this one behind."

Lucinda's eyes widened. "Do you think he'll come back for it?"

"Probably not," I said, more to calm her down than anything. "Besides, even if he realizes it's gone, he won't necessarily remember that it came off when he hit you."

Lucinda gripped my arm. "I'm frightened, Simon. I doubt I could survive another attack. It's time we called the police."

I bit my lip as I thought. "I suppose you're right."

She studied my face. "You don't want to."

I nodded. "I'm worried about challenging Raymond. He's evil, Lucinda, and he's clever. He knows every legal loop hole. And what he doesn't know, his lawyer does."

"But we have evidence now."

I sighed. "It may not be enough. I'll call the police and find out if Sergeant Baker's on duty. I spoke to him in the hospital. If I explain it's the same case, they might send him."

"Good idea."

I reached for the phone and dialed 911. As I waited to be connected to the local precinct, I told myself I was doing the right thing. Lucinda needed protection.

The dispatcher said that Sergeant Baker was on duty and would get to Lucinda Davenport's house within the hour.

"Who else do you want to call?" Lucinda asked.

"What makes you think I want to call anyone else?"

She laughed. "The way you're gripping the phone. Besides, that knock on my head hasn't taken away all my ESP."

"I want to call a lawyer I know. I want him here when we talk to Sergeant Baker."

"And afterward, you want to tell him everything."

I nodded. "Someone should know what Raymond's been up to."

"Go and call him. He'll be home."

I gave a start. "The lawyer? But you don't even know who he is."

"Doesn't matter. I know what I know. Call him. Set it all up. I'm going to bed. Wake me when the show begins."

Chapter Nineteen

Forty-five minutes later, Aunt Lucinda and I sat facing Sergeant Baker and Chuck Bayard in the living room. The two men had pulled up kitchen chairs. I handed the bagged evidence to the policeman and explained how I knew it belonged to Craig Averil.

The officer studied the pin through the plastic then fixed his eyes on me. I blinked twice but held his gaze. I refused to glance away. Finally, he turned to Lucinda.

"Do you agree with what your nephew just told me, Miz Davenport?"

Lucinda shrugged and huddled into herself. She looks frail. Tiny. Not much bigger than Lucy. *She's not up for this. We should have left it for tomorrow.*

She spoke softly. "I remember grabbing his jacket, and the pin falling to the floor. I gave the back of it to Simon, and told him to look for the rest."

Sergeant Baker nodded. "Your nephew here is certain your assailant is Craig Averil. Did you recognize him, Ms. Davenport?"

"I don't know any Craig Averil," she snapped. "At least, I haven't set eyes on him in years. If Simon says that's who it was, I've no reason to disbelieve him."

Sergeant Baker nodded and jotted down something in his notepad. He looked up and directed his next question to me.

"What makes you so certain Mr. Averil attacked your great-aunt? I bet plenty of people have these pins. I bet you have one."

I felt the blood rush to my ears. "I do have a pin like that, but you can check the one in the Baggie for fingerprints. I was careful not to touch it."

"You haven't answered my question—a question you said you couldn't answer Thursday night at the hospital."

Chuck was about to speak, but Lucinda got in there first. "I don't like your tone, young man! This is no way to treat an old woman who's been bonked on the head, and her young nephew who's trying to help you find a criminal!"

The officer cleared his throat. "Sorry, ma'am. Simon, why do you insist it's Mr. Averil who attacked your aunt the other evening?"

There was no avoiding it now. I drew a deep breath. "Because I overheard him telling my uncle what he'd done. That's how I knew to come here that night."

"Your uncle being —?"

"Raymond Davenport. I live with him and his wife, Mary. Craig came to visit my uncle Thursday evening."

The policeman looked perplexed. "And why would Mr. Averil come to your uncle's home and confess to a crime he'd just committed?"

"That's speculation," Chuck put in quickly. "How could Simon know why Craig Averil did what he did?"

Sergeant Baker cast an irritated glance at Chuck. "Relax, counselor. Court's not in session. I'm simply trying to get an understanding of what happened and why." He turned to me. "Do you know why Mr. Averil told your uncle he'd assaulted Miz Lucinda – if, in fact, that's what he did?"

Here goes nothing. I felt like I was being shot out of a cannon and would land God knew where. "Because Craig works for my uncle." I suddenly remembered a police procedural TV show I used to watch. "I bet if you checked their bank statements you'd find the financial connection that proves I'm right."

Sergeant Baker found that funny. When he finished laughing, he said, "You still haven't explained what I asked."

I shrugged. "My uncle wants to build condos on land the local kids use as ball fields. He's acting as though he owns the land, but the truth is, it belongs to all Davenports."

"I'm opposed to the condos," Lucinda said. She yawned. "My nephew Raymond will go to any extreme to get what he wants."

"Then you think he's behind this?" Sergeant Baker asked.

"I'm sure he is. Now I'd like to go back to bed. I can hardly hold up my head."

I stood. "I'll help my aunt to her bedroom."

When I returned to the living room, Chuck and Sergeant Baker were conversing in low voices. They fell silent as I approached.

"If you've nothing to add, I'll be going," the policeman said.

I've plenty to add, but not yet. Aloud, I asked, "are you going to arrest Craig?"

"I'll talk to him and to your uncle."

I shuddered to think of how that would play out. "They'll deny it, of course."

Sergeant Baker picked up on my concern. "Mr. Davenport's your guardian. If you're worried he'll mistreat you after he learns of your part in all this, maybe you'd be better off staying with friends for a while. Or I could arrange for you to go to a Safe House."

I gave a bark of laughter. "Don't worry, Sergeant Baker. My uncle won't hurt me—at least not severely. You can be sure of that."

For the first time that evening, the policeman looked shocked.

"If the man's abusing you in any way – "

I shook my head. "He isn't." *Not in any believable way, he's not.* "Don't worry about me. I can take care of myself."

"I worry when a minor tells me he can take care of himself."

"My Aunt Mary's okay," I said. "And my uncle's practically bedridden."

Officer Baker didn't look convinced. "Promise you'll call the station if you need my help. Any time, day or night."

Touched, I said I would. I saw the policeman out and returned to the sitting room. I gave Chuck a half smile as I sat down. "Now for the complete version."

I started with the death of my parents and talked for a full hour. Chuck listened in rapt attention. When I finished, he shook his head.

"Incredible! That's the wildest story I've ever heard in my life."

Was he calling me a liar? "Don't you believe me?"

Chuck grimaced. "I'd like to. I think you're a great kid and I know you've been through more than any kid should have to endure, but all this – about the murders and your uncle wanting to take over your body. It sounds like science fiction."

I covered my face with my hands. If I couldn't convince Chuck who liked me, no adult would believe what I said about my uncle.

"If you could only give me a shred of evidence," Chuck urged. "Something I can see."

"I did that," I said dryly. "I gave the camp pin to Officer Baker."

"Think!" Chuck ordered.

He's on my side, but he's having trouble wrapping his mind around all the woo-woo stuff. What can I tell him? What can I prove?

I had it. "Go into the kitchen," I told Chuck, "and whisper something."

"What should I whisper?" Chuck asked, already on his way.

"I don't care. Anything. Just whisper it, then come back here."

Chuck returned to the sitting room a minute later.

"You said you're sorry, but you'll have to leave soon because you have a date."

Chuck's face lit up. "Right! You heard it all the way from the kitchen?"

I nodded. "I have especially keen hearing. Which is how I heard

Craig tell my uncle he hit Lucinda and left her for dead. That's why I ran here, to my aunt's house."

I drew a deep breath. "I can see in the dark. I can tell you're getting excited, but since I can't read your mind, I can't say about what. These are Davenport traits. My uncle has other talents, none of them good."

I held my breath waiting for Chuck's mind to digest what I'd told him.

"All right. I believe you, though, for your sake, I was hoping it wasn't true. I always figured those tales about your family were just—stories."

"You've heard stories?"

Chuck smiled. "Sure. Remember, I grew up in Buckley. The Davenports have always had an unsavory reputation. One of your relatives killed his wife, but the jury failed to convict him." He laughed. "According to my grandfather, Randolph Davenport spooked the jurors. They were too afraid of his curse to convict him of murder.

"Years ago there was talk of suspicious deaths, even among family members. Tales of how some Davenports killed innocent people to keep themselves alive. No proof of any of this, but for years any unexplained death was laid at a Davenport's doorstep. As I said, that was many years ago."

I shuddered. "Does everyone in town know these stories?"

"Probably not since they're old stories. Over the years, lots of older folk have died or moved away."

"Do people suspect that my uncle's been killing these girls?"

"I doubt it. We've had a large influx of new people moving into town. For example, your friends, Andy and Pol, moved here eight years ago. And they know Raymond Davenport as a pillar of the community. He's been voted Buckley's Citizen of the Year three times. Who would suspect him of killing young girls to prolong his life?"

I grimaced. "And we've no way of proving that's exactly what he did."

"Sad to say, you're right. But right now I'm more concerned about you, Simon. I can't say if he has the power or the ability to take over your body, but I don't like to think of what might happen to you when he tries it."

"Don't worry about me! I'm getting out of here!"

"Where are you going?"

The million dollar question. "I'm not sure, but I can't stay in Buckley. I want you to know what's been happening so you can tell the police about it when I'm gone. Unless you're worried they'll lock you in the loony bin."

"I'd like you to let me decide when's the best time to tell the police all this."

I shrugged. "Sure."

"The police need hard evidence in order to charge your uncle with a crime."

"I've no proof of what he's done. As for taking over my body—they'll laugh and tell me to stop reading Stephen King."

Chuck nodded. "You're probably right."

He left shortly after, having extracted my promise that I wouldn't leave Buckley without talking to him first. I punched in Lucy's phone number and got the message I'd expected—her phone had been disconnected. I looked in on Lucinda. She was sound asleep, breathing normally. There was nothing for me to do but head back to the lion's den.

Chapter Twenty

I was about to unlock the front door when my smartphone rang. Lucy! I yanked it from my pocket and dropped it on the front step.

"Hello?"

"Simon, this is your Aunt Grace."

"Aunt Grace." Thoughts ricocheted inside my head. Was she calling to ream me out again? Or maybe she'd changed her mind about letting me go with them to England.

"Lucy's gone! He's taken her!"

My heart leaped to my throat. "Who did?"

"You know who! And it's your fault! You led them straight to Lucy!"

I gasped. Raymond must have put a trace on my phone! How stupid I'd been, thinking I could outwit my uncle! My body trembled as questions and self-recrimination blitzed my brain. I tried to speak, but my thoughts were too jumbled to emerge in coherent sentences. *Calm down!* I swallowed and tamped down my terror as best I could.

"What happened? When?"

Aunt Grace sounded as frantic as I felt. "Not ten minutes ago I heard knocking on the door. I told Lucy to go into the bedroom. Someone started to work on the locks. A minute later two men rushed into our apartment. Big men. They pushed past me and headed for the bedroom." Her voice trembled as she continued. "They found Lucy cowering in the closet. One snatched her up like a bundle of wash and took her away." Aunt Grace gave a loud wail, "And I stood there doing nothing. I did nothing to stop them."

"Did you call the police?"

"Of course. I told them who was responsible. No matter how I explained things, they thought I was embroiled in some kind of custody battle. They promised to investigate my charges against Raymond Davenport." She made a disparaging sound. "They probably think I'm a raving lunatic."

"I've been out all day, Aunt Grace. I'll talk to Raymond and make him tell me what he's done with Lucy."

I heard sobbing, then Aunt Grace exclaimed, "Don't bother, Simon! You're probably in cahoots with him."

I felt the blood drain from my head. "I am not! What an awful thing to say!"

"It's the only thing that makes sense. You visit Lucy and suddenly she's kidnapped. Your uncle's evil. He's corrupted you, too."

"He hasn't!" I insisted, even as I wondered if she was right. All those Raymond memories and feelings. Had my uncle managed to change me so that I wasn't aware of what I'd become? Had I'd gone to visit Lucy, knowing all the while I was being followed? That Raymond was tracing my phone calls?

Of course not! I couldn't live with myself if this were true.

"I love Lucy!" I shouted. "She's the only family I have. When all this is over, we're going to be together."

"My sister asked me to keep Lucy safe and I failed," Aunt Grace said. "God knows what that monster wants with her. She's only a little girl."

My blood froze at the thought of what my uncle wanted with Lucy. "I'm going to save her," I declared with more force than I felt.

"Call me as soon as you know anything." She rattled off a number.

"I will, Aunt Grace. I'm sorry."

She hung up. I squeezed my eyes shut. I wouldn't cry. I wouldn't waste my energy on emotions. I had to act now. While there was still a chance to save my sister's life.

I stormed into the house, determined to confront my uncle. The center hall was as cool and dim as a cave. Silence reigned, but for the whirring of the AC system. As far as I could tell, nobody was home.

Out of habit, I peered into the den. Aunt Mary sat slumped on the couch, her head falling onto her chest as if she were fast asleep. Or dead!

I knelt down beside her. "Wake up, Aunt Mary! Wake up!"

She stirred and struggled to open her eyes. "What is it?" she muttered, her voice slow and thick. Her eyelids clamped shut again.

My heart lurched with pity. Raymond had hypnotized Aunt Mary, knocking her out. Why now? Of course! Lucy. Had my uncle taken my sister to be his latest victim?

"Raymond!" I screamed as I flew up the stairs to my aunt and uncle's bedroom. Empty, as I'd expected. Where was my uncle? The last time I'd seen him—was it actually this morning?—he'd been weak and sickly. Since then Lucy had been kidnapped, and my aunt was reduced to a zombie. Why? What was Raymond plotting now?

Frantically, I tore from room to room, hoping to find him, or at least a sign of where he'd gone. Downstairs, his office was in orderly condition. The top of the desk was bare except for his computer. I turned it on but was unable to open any files without the necessary password.

I typed in various words, a few number and letter combinations, then gave up in disgust. Raymond was too cunning to use a password that was obvious. If only I'd been cunning enough to erase evidence of my phone calls to Lucy. If only I hadn't left my phone at home on Friday! I checked the garage. My uncle's BMW was gone. No doubt he'd gone to where the men had taken my sister.

I flexed my fists in futile anger. I had to save Lucy, but hadn't the vaguest idea who to call, where to go. Aunt Grace had already called the police, which would lead nowhere. I was useless. Worse than useless, because I'd led Raymond right to Lucy.

I had no idea how long I sat mulling at the kitchen table, when I heard a key in the lock. I raced to the hallway, intent on wringing the truth from my uncle.

"There you are, Simon!" Raymond wore a white short-sleeved shirt and casual pants. He looked a good deal healthier than he had earlier in the day.

"Where's my sister?"

Raymond shot me an amused smile. "I see news travels fast."

I wrapped my hands around his neck and squeezed. "Tell me."

He showed no surprise at my actions. "Release me, Simon, and we'll talk."

"Like hell we will! I know what you do to little girls!" I squeezed tighter.

Raymond coughed. His face turned red but his eyes never left mine. They glowed like burning coals. "Drop your hands, if you hope to hear about Lucy."

"You deserve to die!"

"I nearly did yesterday, but today I'm fit as a fiddle."

Reluctantly, I released my choke hold on my uncle.

"That's better." Raymond rubbed his neck. "We'll talk in my office." It was an order, not a suggestion.

He turned on the light and closed the door behind us. He gestured to me to sit down. I didn't move.

"I'm both amused and annoyed to see you try to thwart me. Pleased, because courage and ingenuity are positive personality traits that will remain when I take over your body." Raymond frowned. "I'm annoyed because you've thrown minor snags into my plans. I need all my energy

150

to realize my greatest achievement—becoming Simon Porte."

A chill ran through my body. "That's not going to happen! The police know all about you. I've told them Craig went after Lucinda on your orders. They'll be coming round to question you both."

"So I've been warned," Raymond said, not at all perturbed. "And you will have the unhappy chore of informing whichever officer comes to speak to us that you're very sorry, but you misunderstood what you thought you'd heard."

"I will not!" I stepped toward him, and felt a twinge of satisfaction when he inched back.

But my sense of gaining the upper hand was short-lived when he waved his hand dismissively. "Sit down, Simon, and we'll talk about Lucy."

Disheartened, I obeyed. Raymond sat beside me. "You never told me your sister was fortunate to survive the accident that took your parents. I admit, this came as a huge surprise."

"You checked my phone. I should have erased everything."

"Don't beat yourself up, as they say. I knew of every call you made, every website you visited."

"How could I have been so stupid?"

Raymond slapped me on the knee. "On the contrary. You're a very intelligent lad, but you've set yourself up against a man more than three times your age. A businessman wise to the ways of the world."

"You're a murderer! You killed my parents—your own brother and sister-in-law!"

Raymond had the gall to look as if he were sorry. As if he really cared about anyone other than himself. "That was a tragedy. But they never would have let you come to me, would they? And I need you more than I need anyone on earth."

"You don't need my sister!" I shouted.

"Please keep your voice down," Raymond said. "Your Aunt Mary may wake up and wonder why you're so angry with me."

"I bet she knows! Which is why you hypnotized her, or whatever you do to the poor woman."

Raymond turned away, but not before I'd caught an expression of remorse on his face. Not that it mattered. Nothing mattered except convincing him to set Lucy free.

"Lucy's important to you, isn't she?" Raymond said.

"Yes."

"She's safe and comfortable in a home not far from here. I rescued her from your rather severe aunt because I know you both want to be together. And you shall. You shall!"

I stared at him. "You're not planning to harm her?"

"Of course not," he chided me. "What an idea! But you haven't been very cooperative with me, have you?"

Dread pressed down on me, snuffing out all hope. What was coming was worse than anything so far.

"I think you know what I've been working toward ever since you came to Buckley."

"You're trying to take over my body," I mumbled.

"Not trying. Laying the groundwork. But you fight me every inch of the way. And you're strong. Very strong."

My gasp of horror made him smile. "Ah, you've caught the gist of where this is going. I expect you'll be more cooperative from now on." His smile grew wider. "If you want your sister to live."

I buried my face in my hands. It was over. Raymond was far more clever than I could ever hope to be. He'd take over my body, and then he'd kill Lucy.

"Don't fret, Gregory." Raymond turned his chair so he could face me. I wrinkled my nose against his medicinal breath. "Relax, my boy. We've time for a short session before your Aunt Mary wakes up and starts dinner."

Chapter Twenty-One

The image of a young girl entered my mind. I watched the plastic tube-like device slip from her mouth as her face contorted into a death mask. I shook my head vehemently to erase the sight and broke my uncle's spell.

"You're a monster!" I pushed him away, horrified that I'd left my mind open to his evil intentions.

Raymond grabbed my arm. "Calm yourself, Gregory. You must learn how to acquire your source's life force when needed."

"Kill a girl, you mean."

His grip grew tighter. "Let's not argue over semantics. There's Lucy's welfare to consider."

"How do I know you won't kill her."

Raymond pursed his lips. "I thought I'd made myself clear. You cooperate, Lucy goes free."

"Why should I believe you?"

Raymond released his hold on me. "Tsk, tsk. Such little trust. And what if I allowed you to speak to her on the telephone? Would you believe me then?"

"How often?"

"How often!" Raymond repeated, incredulous. "You'll talk to her once!"

I forced a laugh. "Big deal. That's supposed to reassure me."

He gave a snort of exasperation. "All right. Every few days starting tomorrow. Satisfied?"

"No! Every day, morning and night."

"I'll agree to once a day, as long as you're cooperative."

I grimaced, dreading what I was agreeing to. "All right."

"Good. Let's get back to work. Keep your eyes open, understand?"

"Yes." But this time I was ready. I closed his mind and let my eyes wander. I glanced around the office. Anywhere but into my uncle's intense gaze.

"Look into my eyes!"

I obeyed and struggled not to lose consciousness. How long could I endure my uncle's infusions? Regardless of how hard I fought to close myself off, some of Raymond's memories and personality managed to seep into my brain.

"We'll try something different this time."

He seemed to be speaking to me from a great distance. Was I asleep? Unconscious? I felt detached. Not connected to anything. Like a balloon drifting through space.

"Simon, where are you?" a voice demanded. "I need to speak to you."

I gave a jolt and sat up. Aunt Lucinda was calling to me.

"I'm here. Raymond's giving me an infusion."

"Well, stop it!"

"I can't. He's—"

"Concentrate! Don't break the connection!" Raymond instructed, unaware that he was interrupting my conversation with Lucinda.

I blinked as I came out of the trance. What had just happened? Had I succumbed to a strong infusion?

My uncle stood over me muttering curses.

"Tell him you're tired and you can't do this any more today."

"He won't believe me."

"Tell him!" Lucinda ordered. "Pretend what he's done has taken effect and we'll pray to God that it hasn't."

I forced a smile on my face. "Phew! That was awesome."

"Really?" Raymond stepped back, all smiles. "Tell me what you experienced?"

"It was like floating on a cloud." I paused to think. What traits did my uncle want to transfer to his new life? What skills? The ability to wheel and deal. To influence and make money. "I saw some kind of business transaction."

"Excellent" my uncle exclaimed, patting my arm. "Can you remember any details?"

Instead of answering, I let my head fall to my chest and pretended to doze off. My uncle shook me.

"Wake up, my boy! Wake up"

I kept my eyes shut, until the touch of his hands on my face made me shudder. I brushed them away and let out a gigantic yawn. "I'm exhausted. I need to rest."

"Of course, Gregory."

I glared at him. Raymond looked nervous as he backed up until he bumped into the desk. "I've told you often enough—my name is Simon. If you don't use it, I won't help you."

"Yes, yes. Anything you say, my boy. Good-bye." Raymond slipped out of the office, an expression of satisfaction on his face.

I raced up to my room, slammed the door shut, and tumbled onto my bed. Wow! Where on earth did that last bit come from? It had scared the bejeezus out of Raymond, though it had pleased him as well. Were my own powers developing and growing stronger? Or were Raymond's infusions starting to work?

Lucinda, who hadn't left, laughed maniacally in my head. "You acquired a touch of Raymond and gave it back to him like he deserves," she said when she'd calmed down. "Though I shouldn't be laughing. You mustn't let him do this to you. It's dangerous, Simon. Leave that house now."

"I can't. He has Lucy."

"Raymond has Lucy! When did this happen?"

I told her about Aunt Grace's call and my uncle's conditions. "So you see, I have no choice but to do pretty much what he says," I finished.

"Of course you have a choice!" she snapped back. "If you let those transformations of his take effect, how will you save your sister?"

"Ouch."

"Face facts if you want to beat that scoundrel. Come over here. I'll teach you a few more tricks to outfox that evil nephew of mine."

The cloud of doom began to lift. "Do you think you can find Lucy?"

"What did he tell you? What do you know?"

"That she's safe in a house close by, and a woman's looking after her. Oh, and I'll be able to speak to her tomorrow."

"Contact me as soon as you're speaking to her. I might get a sense of her location."

"You're the best, Lucinda!"

"Come over here now!"

She was gone before I'd remembered to ask how she was feeling.

A door slammed. I peered out the window. A minute later Raymond was driving down the street. Was he going to see to Lucy or to give Craig more homicidal assignments?

Aunt Mary called to me as I came downstairs. I grimaced. I'd hoped to leave before she awakened.

"Hello, Aunt Mary. How are you feeling?"

She was sitting up on the den couch, smoothing back her hair. "I must have fallen asleep. Do you know what time it is?"

I gazed at her with pity. Did she know her husband had hypnotized her? Or why? "It's a little after five. I'm going out."

"Oh, dear. So late? I'm about to start preparing dinner."

"I'm not sure I'll be home in time for dinner. If I'm not, you can leave my food in the fridge. I'll heat it up when I get home."

Aunt Mary nodded but made no move to get up. I started for the door then turned back. These were desperate times and required desperate measures. I sat down beside my aunt and took her hand in mine.

"Aunt Mary, you weren't taking a nap. Uncle Raymond hypnotized you."

She shook her head, clearly upset. "Don't be silly, Simon. Why would he do a thing like that?"

"Because he does terrible things, things you wouldn't approve of."

Her eyes opened wide. "You mustn't say that! Your uncle's a good man. He's a pillar of the community. Why, he sits on every important committee in Buckley."

I patted her hand. "We both know he's evil through and through. He commits awful crimes. When you tell him to stop, he hypnotizes you so you'll forget. Only you can't forget, can you?"

I watched as opposing forces waged war inside Aunt Mary. Finally, she groaned and covered her face in her hands. "I'm so ashamed. I'm sorry I didn't protect you." She shook her head in despair. "I can't stop him. He defeats me every time."

"We'll stop him," I said.

She released a deep sigh. "How? You're just a boy. Soon—soon—"

So she knew what her husband was planning. Knew and had argued against it, which was why she kept getting zonked.

"Do you want to help me?"

Aunt Mary nodded.

"Then keep out of his way. Don't argue or give him a reason to hypnotize you. And don't tell him we've talked about it."

"Of course not." She gave me a sad smile. "I may be a fool for staying with him all these years, but I'm not stupid."

Chapter Twenty-Two

L ucinda's neighbor was leaving my aunt's house as I arrived. She was a stout, middle-aged woman with short iron-gray hair that she wore like a helmet. She looked me up and down before giving me a smile that was amazingly kind.

"So you're the nephew she's so fond of."

"I'm Simon," I said, feeling both embarrassed and pleased.

"Martha Barrister here. Your great-aunt has suffered quite a blow to her system. Keep her calm. Don't let her get agitated as she's wont to do."

"I'll do my best, Ms. Barrister," I said, knowing my chances of keeping Lucinda calm were as good as my turning Raymond into a frog.

"Call me Martha. And stay tough. It's for Lucinda's own good." She smiled again. "I left some chicken soup on the stove. Heat it up when she says she's hungry."

I thanked Martha and went inside.

"It's about time you got here," Lucinda complained as I entered her bedroom.

I stopped her from climbing out of bed. "I think Martha would rather you stay there."

"Martha," Lucinda echoed, her tone mocking. But she settled back under the covers and patted an empty space for me to sit beside her. "Now, tell me everything that transpired. I want details."

I told her, including my conversation with Aunt Mary. Lucinda nodded her approval. "Good. She's not on Raymond's side. I often wondered where she stood."

"I told her not to rile him up and get herself hypnotized."

Lucinda rubbed her chin. "And maybe she can be of some help. We need all the help we can get. Have the police questioned Raymond about Craig Averil?"

I nodded. "He backed up Craig like we knew he would. But my Aunt Grace told the police in her town that Raymond had Lucy kidnapped."

"There's no proof Raymond's behind Lucy's abduction. No proof of anything against my nephew, your slimy uncle."

I pounded the mattress with my fist. "So what good is their questioning him? He'll deny everything and the cops will think we're all nuts."

"Accusations are coming from too many sources for the police to ignore them. Eventually they'll have to take action," Lucinda said calmly.

I jumped up and glared at her. "Eventually! We have to do something now! Lucy's his prisoner. Raymond says I have to cooperate when he does his infusions or he'll do—God knows what to Lucy!"

"Sit down and calm yourself." Lucinda was unusually composed. "I told you I'd help and I will."

I sat down. "How?"

She smiled, clearly pleased with herself. "Let's start with you. When you close your mind to Raymond, I want you to leave it a bit open. Like a door ajar. Do you know what I mean?"

I nodded. "I think so. But I hate when he gets inside my head and deposits his gruesome memories. Before I had this awful image of a young girl gasping for breath. She was dying."

"Is the image as vivid now?"

"It's faded a bit, but I can't forget the terror in her eyes. I don't want his thoughts in my head! I can't stand to think the way he does! And I will if he keeps this up like he means to."

"Simon, look at me."

I faced her. Lucinda gripped my wrist. "Listen to me! After each infusion session, you will erase his handiwork. It's a process of visualization, of nullifying his imprint. You must stay awake. It will take all your effort, but you mustn't fall asleep. Can you do that?"

"Yes."

"Make sure that you do. An infusion will exhaust you. You mustn't allow yourself to fall asleep. His imprints will settle into your mind if you do."

I shuddered. "I'll be careful. Now what about the visualization?"

Lucinda went through the procedure with me, making sure I understood every step along the way. Then we went through it again.

"Do you still remember the image of the dying girl?"

I nodded. "As though it were a picture in a book. Her fear, the awfulness of watching her die, is gone."

"Good." Lucinda's smile turned into a yawn.

"You're tired," I said. "I should let you rest."

"I'll rest when I'm done. On to Part B."

"Part B?" I asked.

Her expression turned sly. "Just as important as keeping Raymond out of your head is making him believe he's succeeding. Give him some of his own back. Backtalk, sass—whatever you kids call it these days."

I laughed. "Kind of like when Hansel kept sticking out a chicken bone so the witch would think he and his sister were too were skinny to eat."

Lucinda grinned. "Exactly."

I shuddered. My example was too close for comfort.

"As for Lucy," Lucinda said, "when you speak to her, make use of your keen sense of hearing. Take note of every background sound you hear."

"I will."

"While you and she are talking, instruct her silently to tell you where she is. Repeat this again and again."

My mouth fell open. "You think Lucy has special abilities?"

Lucinda grinned. "Let's find out. She's a Davenport, isn't she?"

"Yes, but Lucy and I never communicated that way."

"You never had to. Did you know of your special abilities before you came to Buckley?"

I thought a bit. "I only knew my senses were extra-keen. I had no idea of the extent of my abilities until you told me. Lucy's only nine, and she's all alone."

Fear for my sister filled my chest until I could hardly breathe. I wanted to race around the room so the pent up energy could escape. I felt like a pressure cooker about to explode.

Lucinda's eyes bore into mine. "Take deep breaths," she murmured. "Relax. Relax."

I inhaled, exhaled, inhaled, exhaled until my panic attack subsided.

"Simon, you're living through a nightmare right now, but believe me when I tell you the good in this world outweighs the bad. I sense Lucy's talents." Lucinda gave me an impish smile. "After all, your parents named her after me."

Tears burned my eyes. I wiped them away with my sleeve. My head swarmed with a hundred questions I needed to ask her.

"Aunt Lucinda," I began.

Aunt Lucinda was fast asleep.

* * *

Weird doesn't begin to describe how I felt at dinner. My aunt and uncle greeted me as though nothing unusual had taken place earlier in the day. I nodded to them both and took my seat. We passed around the cold salads Aunt Mary had prepared, then sat chewing and swallowing as though we were a normal family sharing an August evening meal.

Raymond was in high spirits. "You look well rested, Simon!" he boomed.

"I took a nap."

He patted Aunt Mary's hand. "And your potato salad is delicious, my dear. As always."

Aunt Mary nodded but avoided his gaze. "I'm glad you like it, Raymond. Have some more."

"Don't mind if I do!" He held out his plate so she could serve him.

We ate in silence until my uncle said, "By the way, I've been rethinking some decisions I've made and plan to change my course of action."

Which decision? I wanted to shout. *The one to keep your niece a prisoner?* Instead, like Aunt Mary, I said nothing.

Our lack of interest irritated Raymond. He tsk-tsked and looked from his wife to me. "Aren't you going to ask about my new plan?"

Aunt Mary managed a small smile. "Of course we want to know, Raymond. What have you decided?"

Instead of answering, he turned his attention to me. "I suppose your friends are still rallying for that town meeting, hoping we Davenports will keep the land as playing fields."

We Davenports! I looked away so Raymond wouldn't see the contempt I felt for him for calling on the family name. Then I remembered Lucinda's instructions and decided to take the offensive.

"What do you care about the meeting? You're the Davenport set on using the land to build condos." I winked. "Are you planning to finish off Lucinda and me, and get all obstacles out of your way?"

A strangling sound came from my uncle's throat. His eyes bulged and his face burned a bright red. He turned to Aunt Mary, expecting her to scold me for showing him disrespect. When she continued to look down at her hands in silence, Raymond found his voice and his outrage.

"Simon, you're a guest in my house! I'll ask you to keep a civil tongue in your head!"

I met his gaze straight on. "Why, Uncle Raymond, I'm only joking—and stating the obvious. You want to build condos. Lucinda and I want to keep the playing fields as they are. We stand in your way."

"Hah! Your great-aunt Lucinda's as crazy as a loon. And you're a minor! You have no vote concerning this matter!"

I regarded him steadily as I spoke. "But I do, Uncle Raymond. As the land deed was drawn up, every Davenport over the age of sixteen has a vote regarding the use of the land. I'll be sixteen in November, three months from now. I think any judge would take that into account."

Raymond made a froglike sound.

I forced myself to smile with as much confidence as I could muster. "Living with you has been rubbing off on me, Uncle. I'm becoming more and more like you each day."

Aunt Mary gasped at my words, but my uncle merely nodded. A minute later he was beaming. "So you are, Simon, so you are. And you are correct about that old legal paper. I've been considering another property for the condos." He gave a disparaging shrug. "One not as well located as the playing fields, but it's a property I myself own."

Now I was puzzled. "Then what do you care about the town meeting? In fact, there's no need for a meeting if you're no longer considering the playing fields as the condo site."

Raymond nodded. "An astute observation, Simon. But the meeting's been planned. Feelings are high, and I don't want to disappoint our fellow townsfolk."

"How can you disappoint them if you don't intend to take away the fields the kids use for soccer and baseball?"

"I choose to make the grand gesture, my boy!"

I shot him a look of disbelief. "What are you talking about?"

Raymond beamed, eager to reveal his plan. "By hosting the meeting with refreshments and agreeing to leave the playing fields as they are, I'll earn myself many brownie points, as we used to say."

"Huh!"

"Come on, Simon, don't act dense. If I concede what the entire town is after, they'll have to cut me slack when I ask for consideration in future business deals."

"Oh," I said. My uncle was back in the world of financial wheeling and dealing, something I knew little about.

"Don't be discouraged," Raymond said kindly. "You'll learn all about my business concerns in time."

"I don't care about your business concerns," I said.

"So you say now," Raymond said, clearly amused. "That will change sooner than you think."

A tremor ran down my spine. My uncle was planning to make his big move. But when? How? He gave off a strong whiff of anticipation. I tried to catch his gaze, but he wouldn't meet my eyes.

"Did you happen to receive an invitation to Melanie Lewis's party?" he asked.

"Melanie Lewis?" I asked, puzzled by the change of subject. "The head of Arts and Crafts at camp?"

"Yes. I understand she's throwing a party and every counselor's been invited."

"Oh, yeah." I'd gotten an email a week ago, inviting me to some get together Sunday evening and had deleted it without giving it much thought.

"I'd like you to go."

"Why? Aren't you afraid I'll tell everyone about your evil ways?"

Raymond burst out laughing. "Try it and see how fast you end up in the psychiatric ward of the local hospital."

"Raymond, don't," Aunt Mary said softly.

Her husband ignored her as if she hadn't spoken.

"Go to the party. Find out what your friends and other people have to say about the upcoming meeting." He winked. "You might even tell them I'll be attending and catering an array of refreshments for the occasion."

I shrugged. "Sure. Fine. Whatever you say."

Raymond nodded his approval then turned to his wife. "Mary, I think it's time to serve dessert."

"Certainly, Raymond."

As I ate my apple cake and vanilla ice cream, I wondered what my uncle was planning. Why did he suddenly want to attend a meeting that had been set up so residents could argue against his plan? I wished I could read his mind. He had something in the works. But what? If Raymond was happy with the way things were going, they were bound to turn out badly for everyone else.

Chapter Twenty-Three

L ate Sunday morning I was in my room, worrying about Lucy when Raymond shouted from downstairs that I was to join him in his office. I took my time about it. Sure, I hoped he was going to talk to me about Lucy, but most likely he had an infusion in mind. Whichever it was, I refused to appear as vulnerable as I felt.

Raymond shut the door behind us and pointed to a chair. I sat down as he went around to his chair and punched in a number on his phone. From my seat, I managed to see where his fingers landed. I memorized the number he was calling. This was great! If he was calling the people who had Lucy, I'd have Chuck check out the number and get the address! Then I realized Raymond was probably calling a throwaway phone, and we'd have no way of tracking the call.

He said a few words to whomever answered, listened, spoke again, then handed me the phone. "Talk to your sister."

I reached for it in a daze. While I'd been thinking and plotting, I'd missed the few words my uncle had exchanged with Lucy's captor, along with the chance to hear the person's voice.

"Hello, Lucy," I said as I began my silent mantra: *Where are you, Lucy? Where are you?*

"Is that really you, Simon?"

She sounded timid. Terrified. As if she'd been crying. "Yes, it's me, Gretel." *Where are you, Lucy? Where are you?*

"Come and get me! Make them take me to you!"

"I hope to visit you soon. Are you all right?"

"Of course I'm not all right!" She burst into tears.

Raymond tapped my shoulder. "Tell her to behave and she'll come out of this all right."

"Lucy, try to be brave. Like in the witch's house." *Where are you?*

"That's only in a story." *I'm in a barn. On a farm.*

Good girl! I exhaled then coughed so my uncle wouldn't notice my excitement. I could communicate with Lucy the same way I did with Lucinda!

"The story came out all right in the end, didn't it?" I said. "We'll be together soon."

Raymond yanked the phone out of my hand while Lucy was speaking. "Enough." He pressed the "off" button to disconnect the call.

I scowled. "You could have waited till we were finished."

"No, I couldn't. It's time for a little session."

His smile made me long to kick him in his paunchy stomach. Instead, I steeled myself to prevent him from gaining all but the smallest access to my mind. When it was over, I pushed past Raymond and stormed up the stairs to my room.

"Lie down and rest," Raymond called after me.

"I'm going out," I shouted over my shoulder. The session had left me disoriented and dizzy. I needed fresh air to stay awake so I could counteract the infusion. Besides, defying Raymond every chance I got helped me keep from going bonkers.

I splashed water on my face, then grabbed my phone and flew back downstairs, eager to leave the house. The office door was closed, which meant my uncle was probably on the phone. I put my ear to the door. He was talking to the person watching Lucy.

"Keep her comfortable." There was a pause, then he said, sounding annoyed, "Of course she can watch TV!"

I sighed, somewhat relieved. It didn't sound like Raymond was planning to hurt Lucy, at least not in the immediate future. I ran through everything I'd learned so far: I had the number of the person's cell phone; they were keeping Lucy in a barn on a farm; the farm had a TV.

"Simon!"

I spun around, my heart in my throat, until I realized Aunt Mary was beckoning to me from the kitchen.

"What's going on?" she demanded. "I know he's up to something awful."

"He took my baby sister."

"Oh!" She pressed her hand against her mouth. "Your sister. I didn't know."

"I found out Lucy was alive and went to see her. He must have had me followed or traced my calls."

Aunt Mary sank into a chair and buried her face in her hands. "I'm so sorry, Simon."

"Not as sorry as I am," I said.

"So that's why John Knowles stopped by this morning. Early, around eight-fifteen, while you were sleeping. They went to have breakfast in the diner, Raymond said. I figured they wanted to talk in private."

"Who's John Knowles?"

"Buckley's police chief. He looked dead serious when he came by. I wonder how he knew what Raymond had done."

"Aunt Grace told the police Lucy was taken and Uncle Raymond was responsible." I made a sound that was no-way polite. "I told a Buckley cop that Raymond sent Craig Averil to kill my Aunt Lucinda, only he's still walking around, a free agent."

Aunt Mary's eyes were the saddest I'd ever seen. "Raymond's a respected citizen. Without proof, no one will believe he's as much as dropped litter in the street."

"I know. Later, Aunt Mary."

She touched my arm. "Simon, you're not really becoming like him, are you? Like you said last night at dinner?"

"No way! I swear."

She gave me a weak smile. "Thank God. I don't think I could bear it."

Outside I started running slowly, relieved that the affects of the infusion were wearing off. I stopped after a few blocks to call Andy.

"Hey, stranger," he greeted me. "What happened to you?" I heard voices in the background.

"What do you mean?"

"I'm talking about yesterday. You never showed up at the pool. Pol said she saw you in the library. You acted weird and took off."

"Yesterday?" *Feels like a hundred years ago.* I suddenly remembered. Lucy had called when I was talking to Pol. "Yeah, I'm sorry. Some family stuff came up, stuff I had to take care of."

Andy's laugh was mocking. "Don't tell me you're growing fond of your uncle?"

I had to be careful since Raymond was probably monitoring my calls. "I just apologized, didn't I? Where are you?"

"At a family barbecue. My mom made Pol and me come." Andy sighed heavily. "It's worse than I expected, and my uncle burned all the hot dogs. At least we'll have some fun tonight."

"You're going to Melanie Lewis's party?"

"Pol and I thought we'd stop by."

"I was thinking of going, but I never got around to RSVPing."

"Melanie won't care. Come by the house around eight and we'll walk over." Andy paused. "Unless—"

My heart started to pound. I was scared, but it was different from my fear for Lucy's safety. "Unless what?"

"Unless you and Pol had a fight and aren't talking. Lately, you guys have been acting weird around each other." Andy exhaled loudly.

"Frankly, I can't deal with all that hostility."

"Pol and I are great!" The blood rushed to my face. "I mean, she's the last person I'd be hostile towards. I'm sorry if she's mad because I had to cut our conversation short at the library."

Andy's voice sounded funny when he said, "You're sure it's family business you had to take care of?"

"Of course. What else?"

"Nothing." He paused, then said, "Oh hell, because my suspicious twin thought it was Tasha who'd called you."

I laughed. "Well, it wasn't. And you can tell Pol that."

I hummed as I set out for Lucinda's house. I had no business feeling happy when my sister was probably crying her eyes out and fearful for her life. But knowing I'd be seeing Pol later on lifted my spirits. Besides, Lucy was okay for now. What's more, she had powers, too. Maybe everything would turn out okay, after all.

Lucinda came to the door. She seemed stronger, and her face no longer looked papery white. She led me to the sitting room and grinned when I told her Lucy figured out they were keeping her in a barn.

"Good girl! We Davenport women are tough and smart." She elbowed me in the ribs. "If you and Lucy can communicate while you're talking on the phone, you can do it any time. Just like you and me."

"But you gave me numbers to use to contact you," I reminded her.

"That's because you and I were virtual strangers. You and Lucy are close siblings, and it worked immediately."

I told Lucinda I'd memorized the number Raymond had called, and there was a TV in the barn where Lucy was being kept.

"Get me a pad and pencil, Simon." She pointed to the small, rickety desk. "We'll write it all down so we don't forget anything."

I waited impatiently while she printed it out painstakingly slow. Then she said, "I'll call your friend, Chuck, and give him this number.

He should be able to track it down."

"I sure hope so," I said, and told her what Aunt Mary had told me.

"So, it turns out Mary Wicker has some gumption, after all," she mused.

I grimaced. "A fat lot of good that's going to do us."

Aunt Lucinda shook the pencil at me. "Don't be so negative, boy! This is all out war. We make use of all the people on our side."

"Like who?"

She chuckled. "Like your lawyer friend, for one. Chuck was stunned when you finished telling your tale, but he believed you."

I shrugged.

"And Sergeant Baker, for another."

"Really? How do you know?"

"He called this morning to find out how I was feeling. He said Craig Averil denied ever coming here, much less knocking me down. Craig said I was a crazy old lady who should be locked up. From the tone of his voice, I knew Sergeant Baker gave more credence to you and me than to Mr. Averil. But without proof, the police can't throw him in jail where he belongs."

"What about the camp pin we gave him? Isn't that proof Craig came into your house and hit you?"

Lucinda sighed. "There were no clear prints. And Sergeant Baker said there are dozens of those pins floating around town."

"Not to mention the police chief is Uncle Raymond's buddy. This morning they went out for breakfast to talk about things."

Lucinda nodded. "John Knowles is as cautious as they come. He'll stick by Raymond until proof of his evil ways is shoved in his face. Then watch him put my slimy nephew behind bars."

"I hope that happens soon. I don't know what Raymond has in mind for Lucy."

"What about your friends, the twins?" Lucinda asked. "Can you count on them to help?"

"I don't know how they can help. They have no idea of what I'm going through. They'd think I was crazy if I told them."

Lucinda met my gaze straight on. "Maybe it's time you put their friendship to the test."

I was on my way home when I realized I'd forgotten to tell Lucinda about Raymond's plan to attend the town meeting and announce his change of plans. But maybe that wasn't important, with everything else going on.

Chapter Twenty-Four

After dinner, I showered and dressed with care. I grabbed a light jacket and kissed Aunt Mary good-bye.

"I hope they won't be serving any liquor to you young people," she said.

"Don't worry, Aunt Mary, I won't touch a drop." I wouldn't, either. I needed a clear head and my wits about me to deal with everything coming down around me.

Outside, the sky was dark and the air felt cool, reminding me that the summer vacation was drawing to a close. Camp ended on Friday. Thursday evening was the town meeting. After Labor Day Weekend, the new school year began. I wondered where I'd be then—attending classes, on the run, or serving as an unwilling host to my uncle. I shook my head vigorously at the last one. No way would I allow my uncle's maniacal plan to succeed.

The only good thing was being able to contact Lucy after I left Lucinda's. Lucy got so excited when she realized we could communicate, I had to calm her down for fear she'd tip off the woman looking after her. Knowing I was only a thought away lessened some of her terror, especially when I said our Great-Aunt Lucinda was helping to rescue her. Our connection grew faint, probably because it was new to Lucy and had worn her out. I told her to sleep as much as she could, and we'd talk again in the morning.

For the first time, I was nervous when I rang the Coltranes' doorbell. Andy let me inside. Clearly, he hadn't taken the trouble to dress for the party. His chinos were wrinkled, and his shirttails hung out of his pants as usual.

He eyed me up and down. "You look all spiffed up."

My ears grew warm. "I showered and put on clean clothes. After all, we are going to a party."

Andy shrugged. "Big deal. I'm in the middle of a game. I hope to get my highest score ever. Be finished in a minute."

I followed him into his bedroom and watched him feverishly attack an army of ghouls on the computer screen, accompanied by howls of rage and shouts of glee. After a few minutes, Andy called over his shoulder, "This will take a while. Why don't you go say hi to Pol. See what she's up to."

"Sure. Why not?" My pulse rate shot up as I followed Andy's suggestion. Pol's door was closed. I took a deep breath and knocked. She opened it a crack and peered out.

"Are you decent?" I asked.

"I'm always decent," she answered, flinging open the door. "Come on in."

"Wow!" I exclaimed. Pol wore a sea-green silk top with spaghetti straps over her jeans and high heels. With her hair caught in an upsweep and her eyelids tinted violet, she hardly looked like the girl I saw at camp every day.

"That's some outfit."

"Think so?" She swirled a silk shawl around her shoulders and struck a pose. Suddenly she looked older.

I swallowed. "You're not wearing that getup to the party."

Offended, Pol wrinkled her nose. "Why? Don't you like my shawl?"

I felt like a rabbit caught in a snare! Whatever I said now would come out wrong. "It's beautiful. But isn't this party kind of casual?"

"Translated I should look as sloppy as my brother?"

"I didn't mean—"

Her face had turned beet red. "Go back to Andy's room. He won't mind your comments about his clothes."

I struggled to find the words that would make things right. "Pol, come on. I only meant—"

But she shooed me out and slammed the door behind me. Totally mortified, I returned to Andy's room.

"She threw you out," Andy said, turning from his game.

"Yeah." I was beginning to wonder if coming tonight was a mistake. "Hey, maybe I'll forget about this party thing."

"Don't be silly," Andy said. "I'll finish this game then we'll stop by there for a while."

"All right," I agreed. Going to this party was better than sitting in my room worrying when my uncle would try another infusion, and mulling about poor Lucy.

Fifteen minutes later, Mrs. Coltrane drove the three of us to the party. Andy sat in the front passenger seat. Pol and I sat in the back. I turned to her several times during the ride, but she kept her eyes forward. I tried to come up with an apology that would get her to talk to me again, but everything that came to mind sounded dumb.

Mrs. Coltrane parked on a street of beautiful homes set back on imposing lawns. I was surprised when she got out of the car and walked with us past several parked vehicles, then up the long driveway leading to the Lewis's home. But as soon as I entered the two-story hall of the enormous house, I realized the party wasn't only for camp people. Guests of all ages filled the four downstairs rooms and spilled outside, onto the large terrace and pool area.

Melanie Lewis dashed over to greet us. I didn't know her very well since I had little contact with the camp's arts and crafts program. She was tall, with long dark hair, and was pretty in a natural outdoorsy kind of way. She hugged the four of us in turn.

"Come on outside," she beckoned with a wave of her hand. "The good food's out there."

An older woman who looked remarkably like Melanie stopped our progress to whisper something in her daughter's ear. She introduced herself as Melanie's mom, hugged Mrs. Coltrane, and led her away.

Andy stood hand on hips, watching the two women disappear from sight. "There goes Mom. She'll probably end up staying until we decide to leave."

Melanie laughed. "And what if she does? Your mother's welcome, as are all our like-minded friends."

We followed Melanie through the sliding glass doors to the back terrace. I tried not to gape at the platters of food set out on long tables. As if that weren't enough, waitresses circulated with trays of hors d'oeuvres.

"Eat something," Melanie offered, "but drink nothing stronger than soda." She laughed. "We don't want the law coming down on us." She waved and sped away.

Andy rubbed his hands as he leered at the banquet before us. "Food, here I come!" he announced, and started filling a plate.

The beat of the soft rock music filled my head. I tingled with nervous energy, aware of Pol at my side.

"I shouldn't have eaten dinner," I said.

"I should have told you there'd be enough food to feed an army," she said.

"That's okay."

I noticed she'd left the shawl at home, probably because of my dumb comment. As far as I could tell, there was no dress code, though most kids our age were wearing shorts or jeans and a shirt; older guests wore dressier outfits.

"I'm glad you're talking to me again," I said.

"Why wouldn't I be?" Her voice dripped with irony.

I was overcome by the wish to tell her everything. "For one thing, I didn't mean to cut you off at the library yesterday afternoon. That phone call was—"

She pressed her finger to my lips. "Later."

"Okay." I took her hand and squeezed it. "Would you like some soda?"

"Root beer, if they have it. If not, Coke. I'll find us a table." Pol pointed to the small tables set around the pool.

I got on line at the table serving drinks and noticed that, aside from the camp counselors, most of the guests were older. I recognized businessmen and women and store owners I'd seen around town. At a table, two members of the town council carried on a heated conversation. Marshall McMahon and Roderick Tunney were my uncle's opponents regarding most issues. They were responsible for setting up the town meeting to discuss the playing fields. I leaned forward, intent on eavesdropping, when someone gripped my shoulder.

"How goes it, Simon?"

"Chuck! Good to see you!"

He eyed me carefully. "I'm glad you're here. Lucinda filled me in on the latest." He lowered his voice. "Sorry about your sister. I wanted to tell you, but I was hesitant about calling the house. Or even your cell phone." He let out a sigh. "From what Lucinda said, your uncle has all bases covered."

I glanced around to see if anyone could overhear our conversation. "My sister's all right for now. I spoke to her."

"Thank God! Your uncle's some piece of work. Pretending to be an upstanding citizen when he's as low as they get."

I told him about the police chief's visit. As I spoke, a tingling feeling ran up my spine. Someone was watching us! I turned casually, in time

177

to see two men step back into the small forest of trees at the rear of the property.

Chuck frowned. "I don't like the sound of this. Jack—Sergeant Baker believed what you and your aunt told him. He's a straight arrow. You can be sure he won't let this matter rest."

I leaned over and whispered to Chuck. "Start laughing."

"What?"

I began to laugh. I moved closer to Chuck and slapped his back. "Laugh, damn it! I'll explain later."

Chuck laughed. From the corner of my eye, I watched the two men speaking, though I couldn't make out their words. They were big, brawny brutes—totally out of place among the relaxed guests. Not wanting them to know I was on to them, I made a silly comment to Chuck. More laughing and back slapping. When next I checked, they'd disappeared. A flash of motion six feet above the ground told me they'd scrambled over the fence.

"Two men were watching us," I told Chuck. "I didn't want them to think we were discussing anything serious."

Chuck looked around. "Where are they? They've no business invading a private party."

"They're gone. Over the fence and probably in some neighbor's yard by now. They work for my uncle."

Chuck eyed me closely. "You're sure about this?"

I frowned. "Positive, though I've never seen either of them before. I've been a fool, assuming Craig Averil's the only goon he has doing his dirty work."

"Craig won't show up here tonight."

"Why not? He's not in jail where he belongs," I said.

"The police brought him down to the station and questioned him, but they had to let him go. He denied he and your uncle were discussing what you claimed they were talking about. Your uncle backed him up."

I grimaced. "Sure. Then how did I know Lucinda was lying near death?"

"As I said, Jack Baker believes you. But he has to deal with his captain, who's a great pal of your Uncle Raymond. They can't hold Averil without evidence of wrongdoing."

"Evidence," I muttered. "We have no proof of anything, do we?"

"We'll get it," Chuck said. "Jack was livid when Lucinda told him about your sister, Lucy. He's checking out the cell phone number you gave your aunt."

At least I had a lawyer and a cop on my side! But it wasn't enough. Lucy was my uncle's prisoner, and the police chief acted like he didn't believe his friend, Raymond Davenport, was capable of committing heinous crimes.

"But you meant something else—didn't you?—when you said Craig wouldn't show up here."

He nodded. "The Lewises and Craig Averil had a falling out over the issue of the playing fields."

"Really? How do you know?"

My answer came as Melanie joined us and slipped an arm around Chuck's waist. "What are you two conspiring about?" she asked, reaching up to kiss his neck.

He pulled her close and nuzzled her cheek. "Business, my dear. Are there any more of those delicious baby lamb chops coming out soon?"

"I'll go check." Melanie winked. "Hurry back to our table, or I might eat them all myself."

"And I'd better get Pol's soda," I said.

"Call if you need me," Chuck said. "Or if you want to talk."

"I will, thanks." I got back on the drinks line, my mind awhirl. Raymond had spies watching me. How many people worked for him? Carried out his evil deeds? Who was the woman looking after Lucy?"

My Coke in one hand, Pol's root beer in the other, I walked toward the table Pol had snagged for us. A hand reached out to stop me. My heart leaped to my throat. Had my uncle's men returned to grab me?

"You're Eddie Davenport's son, aren't you?"

I looked down into the smiling face of one of the two councilmen I'd noticed earlier.

"Yes, I am."

"I'm Marshall McMahon, a high school friend of your dad's. I was terribly sorry to hear what happened to your parents." He gestured to his skinny table mate. "This is Rod Tunney."

I turned from one smiling face to the other. "Pleased to meet you."

"We're both on the town council with your uncle Raymond."

"I know," I said, ready to move on.

"Any chance he'll change his mind about the playing fields?" Ron Tunney asked.

"Hey, no politics now," his friend chided him. "This is a friendly party."

I saw my chance to ruin my uncle's surprise and get back to Pol in one fell swoop. "Turns out my uncle's changed his mind about building condos on the playing fields land."

The men's eyes lit up.

"You don't say!" Marshall exclaimed. "Who would have guessed old Raymond would have a change of heart, especially when he was bound to make a nice bundle of money?"

"Uncle Raymond's planning to come to the meeting Thursday night. He said he'll bring refreshments."

The announcement left both councilmen speechless. "Gotta go," I said. "Nice meeting you."

I found Pol chatting with two girls at the next table. Andy was sitting beside her, chomping away on his pile of food.

"Sorry I took so long," I said as I handed Pol her root beer.

"That's all right." She smiled and sipped her soda.

Andy came up for air. "You gotta try this chicken. It's awesome!"

"I'm not hungry," Pol said, smiling at me.

"Me, neither." I smiled back.

"Wanna dance?" Pol asked.

I sent her a questioning look. She gestured to the dance floor behind us.

"Sure," I said casually, like I wasn't worried how we'd be as partners.

We joined two other couples dancing in slow motion to "Blue Moon," a song my mom used to sing when she straightened up the house. A minute later we were moving totally in sync as I led her around the small dance floor.

I liked holding Pol in my arms. I breathed in the scent of her freshly shampooed hair, her floral perfume. She hummed softly, then sang the words of the song.

"You know the words!" I said, surprised.

She tilted back her head to smile at me. "I like old songs."

"Me, too," I murmured, and pulled her closer.

When the music stopped, she tried to step back but I held her.

"That was nice," I whispered.

"Yes, it was." She remained in my arms.

The music started up, this time a faster, popular song with a great beat. Again, we danced well together as if we'd been attending the same parties since grade school. I wondered if this had anything to do with my extra-keen powers, or simply that Pol was a graceful dancer and required only the slightest direction to follow my lead. No matter. By the time the medley of songs had ended and we stood applauding, I'd come to a decision.

Pol shot me a questioning look as I ushered her from the dance floor. "Let's go for a walk," I said, guiding her along the path that led to the road.

She laughed. "Simon Porte, are you making a move on me?"

"I want to tell you a few things. You may not be laughing when I'm through."

Chapter Twenty-Five

My uncle insisted on an infusion every day. I did my best to block his toxic invasions, but more than the bit Lucinda said to let in infiltrated my brain. They were mostly his memories and his devious ways of doing business. Raymond had a wheeler-dealer's mentality, and didn't balk at making shady deals as long as he came out ahead. I felt grubby after a dose of those thoughts, and took extra care to scour my mind of them as soon as he left.

As much as I hated my uncle, I also harbored a smoldering rage against Craig Averil. The guy was a traitor of the worst kind. He worked with kids the year round. Both his high school students and Shady Brook campers adored him. Their parents trusted him. But if I hadn't stopped him the other night, he would have sent another little girl to her death.

I wondered if I'd be able to control my anger the next time I ran into Craig, or if I'd simply haul back and start swinging. Sure, he had pounds, inches, and twenty-odd years on me, but I was itching for a fight. My mental and physical powers expanded with each infusion. I had no idea if Raymond knew this would happen, and I made sure he didn't find out. I grinned to think that Craig would probably do nothing if I punched him out. He probably had strict orders to keep his hands off me, regardless of how I behaved.

I got my chance to deal with Craig a few days later when he came to the pool to talk to Rick. He glanced at me as I was instructing a few boys at the shallow end of the pool, then walked on as though I were of no importance. He and Rick stood near the diving boards, laughing about some comment one of them had made.

I shook my head in amazement. The guy came across as harmless as any average middle-class guy in his late thirties. What had turned him into someone's killing machine? Was it money? Power? Or had Raymond incriminating evidence of Craig doing something really awful that he threatened to expose if Craig didn't do his bidding?

"Watch me, Simon!" one of my seven-year-olds shouted.

"I'm all eyes, Jimmy!"

"You made it!" I said after Jimmy had dog-paddled across the width of the pool.

I felt eyes watching me. I caught sight of Craig a few feet away, an insolent grin on his face. *He knows about Lucy and he's glad I'm suffering!* A fireball of fury sped through me as I splashed up the three steps and thrust myself in front of him. Astonished, he stepped back. I inched forward until our noses almost touched. I kept my voice low so only Craig could hear. "When Lucy's safe, I'll take care of you!"

He let out a frog-like croak and ran off, a look of terror on his face.

Yay! I silently cheered, though it was a hollow victory. Lucy was Raymond's prisoner and I was his pawn.

My sister sent me messages throughout the day. I told her to pretend she was Gretel and to report everything she could about where she was and the people looking after her. So far, there was only one woman who started out as a witch then turned out not to be mean at all. At first she kept her distance and spoke harshly, but when Lucy couldn't stop crying the first night, the woman sat with her until she fell asleep.

"What does she look like, Luce?" I asked.

"I don't know 'cause she wears a mask, a loose shirt and baggy pants. But I don't think she's fat. And she's not very old. Younger than Mom

184

was."

"What color hair?"

"I don't know. She wears a turban."

When she started to whimper, I told her she was doing a great job and would probably have more to tell me next time. I hoped she couldn't pick up on my disappointment. We had no idea where she was because after the first day, slats were nailed over the windows. And the cell phone number hadn't panned out since it was a disposable phone.

We had to catch a break and soon.

Lucinda seemed very perky as she recovered from her injuries. I hated to think it was because Lucy's kidnapping was an excuse for her to play detective. When I stopped by her house with Pol on Monday night, Lucinda told me she'd contacted Aunt Grace.

"You shouldn't have!"

"Simon, control yourself," Lucinda scolded. "Your aunt's frantic with worry. She's entitled to know what progress we make."

"We haven't made any progress. Besides, Aunt Grace was nasty to me."

"For good reason," Pol pointed out. "She was afraid your uncle would use you to find Lucy."

"That's exactly what happened!" I slammed against the back of the couch, making the springs moan.

"It's too bad the police don't believe your uncle took your sister," Pol said.

"Not officially, they don't," Aunt Lucinda said. "According to Sergeant Baker, Raymond told Chief Knowles your aunt probably blames Lucy's disappearance on him because she's always hated him. But he and Chuck know the truth. They scour the countryside looking for her every free moment they have."

"If only Lucy could tell us more about the woman Raymond has guarding her."

Lucinda smiled. "I think she will in good time."

"In good time," I grumbled. "We don't have time."

Pol squeezed my hand. The vise constricting my heart eased. I reminded myself I had friends. People were out looking for Lucy. I had to stay positive for my sister's sake.

The next day, Lucy contacted me when I was on the bus going to camp. "She has blonde hair, Simon! Her turban slipped and I saw it! And she had an argument with someone late at night when she thought I was sleeping."

My pulse raced so fast, the vein on my wrist started throbbing. "What were they arguing about, Luce?"

"I'm not sure, but a man drove here. It sounded like a small truck or an SUV. At first they talked quietly in the next room. I couldn't make out the words. And then they started arguing. She asked when they were going to let me go. He said something and she started to yell."

I swallowed, afraid I'd give away my fear. Was Craig the man who went there last night? What did he tell the woman that she didn't like? Something bad regarding Lucy?

"Can you remember any words of their conversation, Luce? Close your eyes and try to remember. Anything will help."

"Okay." A minute later, she continued. "She said she didn't bargain for that, whatever 'that' is. I don't know what she was talking about." Lucy began to cry. "But Simon, I know it wasn't good. I don't want to die, Simon. You have to find me and get me out of here!"

My heart pounded so fiercely, I was certain Lucy could hear it thumping away. I had to come across as calm.

"Lucy, cuddle up to this woman. She likes you. The more she likes you, the better she'll protect you." I had an idea. "Ask her to remove one of the slats they nailed over the window so you can see the sunlight—at least while she's in the room with you. If she does, tell me everything you see from your window. Everything! It's important! People are out

186

looking for you, Lucy. You have to do everything you can to help them find you."

"I'll try, Simon. Oh, one more thing. This man said something about a meeting."

"A meeting!" I must have jumped up in my seat because kids were staring. "Anything else?"

"No. I have no idea what they were talking about."

"I just might. You did great, Gretel." I gathered up all the enthusiasm I could muster and said, "we'll get you out of there yet."

* * *

"Don't worry," Lucinda told me that evening when I'd contacted her our usual way. "You're doing a great job of eradicating his influence on your mind. Besides, Raymond's infusions won't go on forever."

"How much longer?"

Lucinda sighed. "I suppose he'll stop once he realizes he'll never be able to subjugate your will and inhabit your body. That old parchment he found can't possibly work."

My blood ran cold. "What old parchment are you talking about, Lucinda?"

I picked up on her sorrow laced with guilt and embarrassment even before she cleared her throat.

"It's my fault Raymond got ahold of that damn piece of paper! A couple of years back he asked to see some of my grandfather's old books and papers. Stuff I'd packed away in a carton in my attic. Raymond said he wanted to write an historical article about our family." She gave a chortle of derision. "I should have known better."

"So that's how he learned about this transformation business! Did other people in your—our—family succeed in taking over someone else's body?"

Moments passed before Lucinda responded. "I doubt it. When I was little, there was talk that my father's cousin Frank tried to carry out a transformation on a boy—a distant relative."

My heart pounded against my ribs. "Did you know the boy?"

"I met him the one time he came to Buckley on a visit with his parents. They lived in the Midwest. Once his parents discovered what was happening, they grabbed their son and drove home. Though, as I said, the transformation didn't work since Frank was still around after the boy left." She hesitated, then added, "Though I heard he took ill and died shortly afterward."

"Frank?"

"No. The boy."

I exhaled loudly. "None of this makes me feel very good."

"I don't mean to frighten you, but I feel obliged to tell you everything I know. And the truth is, I don't believe a transformation is possible."

"Then why does Raymond think it is?"

She sighed. "He took his idea to someone he believed could help him. A sorcerer, he called him. He bragged that this sorcerer was going to make it work, even if our relative couldn't."

"Oh." I felt as deflated as a burst balloon.

"Simon, it can't work!" Lucinda insisted. "Please believe me! Yes, Raymond can infuse his ideas and his memories into your mind, but only temporarily. And he can't take over your body."

"You don't know that."

"Raymond would need the life force of many, many people to transform himself into you."

"I get the feeling he's planning his big move. I think it has something to do with Thursday night's meeting. Remember, Lucy heard the woman and a man mention a meeting."

Lucinda thought a minute. "In that case, we have to get Lucy away and safe before Thursday night."

"Yeah." My heart plunged to my feet. "That's what I was afraid of."

* * *

As soon we finished eating lunch on Wednesday, Pol tugged my arm. "Let's go for a walk."

Andy let out a groan. "Ugh! You love birds are making me ill."

I grinned, though I figured Pol had something else on her mind. "Wait till it strikes you, old pal. Your life won't be the same."

"I won't let it happen to me," Andy boasted.

"Right," I said. I tossed my lunch trash in the garbage can and followed Pol outside.

"What's up?" I asked when we were walking hand-in-hand along one of the more secluded paths.

"Let's go bowling tonight."

"Bowling?" I stared at her in disbelief. "With everything going on? Lucy's God knows where. I'm about to be served up to zombie-hood."

Pol placed a hand over my mouth. She let me kiss her palm, then gently removed it to set both hands on my shoulders. "That's precisely why we're going bowling tonight. That is, if your uncle lets you out."

"Oh, I'll get out if I want to. Raymond wants me happy. He thinks a happy Simon is a cooperative Simon. He doesn't worry that I'll tell people what he's doing to me because no one will believe me. No one will stop him. And you know what? He's right. No one *will* stop him. So to answer your question, I can go bowling if I like."

I laughed like a maniac until Pol started to shake me.

"Calm down, Simon. Bowling will be good for you. Lucy and Lucinda can reach you wherever you are. And you need to keep busy so you won't worry so much."

I pulled her close. "I can think of a few other things we can do to distract me."

Pol kissed my neck, sending chills up and down my spine. God, she was sexy, in a quiet kind of way. A private way. "We've plenty of time for that, after this is settled. Let's get through tonight."

I returned to the subject that had been bothering me these last few days. "You agree he's planning something for the meeting?"

"I do," Pol said, "but I can't figure out what it is, either." As though reading my thoughts, she added, "and I didn't mention any of this to Andy."

I laughed. "I can't picture Andy wrapping his mind around what I've been living through. It's weirder than the games he plays on his computer. You're sure he doesn't suspect anything?"

Pol shook her head. "He thinks I've gone crazy over you and simply can't think straight."

"Can you think straight?" I murmured, nibbling her ear.

She shrugged, making us both laugh. We kissed for what seemed like minutes, then pulled apart to gaze into each other's eyes.

"I'm crazy about you, too," I told Pol.

Pol winked. "I'll take that as a yes regarding bowling tonight."

Chapter Twenty-Six

T hursday morning at breakfast, Raymond told me to stay home from camp. "I've made your excuses to Craig. Relax. Take it easy." He winked. "You came in late last night from your date with Pol Coltrane. You must be exhausted."

"What are you talking about? I'm fine," I said, alarmed at this latest development. "I'm not tired at all," I lied.

My uncle's phony laugh put me on even higher alert. I wanted to get up and race out of the house, run far from Buckley and never come back.

"You sound anxious. I've something that will help you relax." He held up a small bottle of pills.

"No, thanks."

"Whatever you say. But don't tell me you're going to turn down a day off from camp."

I suddenly remembered Lucinda's advice to pretend I was falling under his influence. I yawned. "Actually, I am kind of tired. I wouldn't mind catching a few more z's."

I downed the rest of my milk, dashed upstairs, and threw myself on my bed. I closed my eyes and pretended to sleep so Raymond wouldn't get another chance to coax me to take one of his pills. Some ten minutes later I heard him open my bedroom door. His breath came in hoarse gasps after the exertion of climbing the stairs. His heart condition was growing worse.

I lay under the covers, feeling as vulnerable as a baby chick while Raymond hovered over me, no doubt thinking hellish thoughts. I longed to jump up and shove the monster out of my room, but my good sense won out and I remained where I was. In order to survive, I had to outwit my uncle. I made the snoring sounds I'd perfected when I was seven, and turned on my side.

It worked. My uncle murmured, "Sleep well, Gregory. We've a busy evening before us. I wish I could sleep too, but I've business to attend to. Tonight we undertake our transformation. Soon I'll be inside your healthy body. I'll be young again, in the prime of life. Won't that be fun!"

The moment he left, I sprang out of bed. Gone was the last remaining hope that my uncle didn't mean to annihilate me. The transformation was scheduled to take place tonight. I had no idea how, but if the little girls' murders were anything to go by, it involved devastation and death.

I trembled as I considered all possibilities, one more horrific than the next. Had Raymond ordered Lucy's kidnapping because he regarded her life force—that of a young Davenport girl—a necessary factor of the transformation?

What did this evening's town meeting have to do with it? Last night I'd told Pol to stay home in case my uncle meant to harm everyone attending. But she'd merely laughed and said that as evil as Raymond Davenport might be, he couldn't kill off a room full of people.

Or could he?

"Simon?"

It was Lucy. "Hi, Luce. Are you okay?"

"I guess." She sounded down.

"Any luck with the lady removing one of the slats from the window?"

"She pulled one out last night so we could see the stars."

"That's a start. It sounds as though she likes you."

"I guess. She told me to call her Romie."

I grinned, suddenly optimistic. "That's great, Lucy! I'll pass the name on to the rescue people. It's an unusual name."

Lucy gave a snort of exasperation "I don't know if it's her name, Simon. It's what she told me to call her."

"Sorry. Anything else, Luce?"

That man came again last night and they screamed at each other. When Romie came into my room, she was crying. She said she never figured to get into something this deep. She said she thought it was a custody battle." Lucy paused, then asked, "What's a custody battle, Simon?"

"When parents are getting divorced and they both want to keep the kids."

"Oh."

She sounded so sad, I had to cheer her up. "You're doing great, Luce. Romie likes you. She's sorry she got herself in the situation of keeping you a prisoner."

I drew a deep breath. "Did you ask her to take down a slot?"

"I didn't get a chance. She was so upset, she brought in my food and left."

We're running out of time! "Ask her to take down a slat. Tell her you want to see the sun. Cry. Whatever you think will work. Then look outside and tell me everything you can see. Got it?"

Some of my terror must have seeped through because Lucy began to sob. "Come and get me, Simon."

"I will, Gretel. We have friends looking for you. They'll rescue you as soon as you can give them an idea where this barn is located."

"All right." She sounded as dejected as I felt. "I'll try."

"Good girl."

I contacted Lucinda to let her know the latest. "Raymond's planning the transformation tonight. I've no idea if that's before, during or after the town meeting."

"And Lucy? Has she learned anything new?"

I told Lucinda about the argument Lucy had overheard.

"They have to find her before the meeting begins!" Lucinda said. "Whatever Raymond has up his sleeve involves you and Lucy."

My body temperature plummeted, as if I'd been dunked in frigid water. Lucy was in grave danger. And so was I.

Lucinda must have picked up this last thought. "Trust me, Simon, your unscrupulous uncle isn't capable of any transformation where you're concerned. For one thing, your own powers have grown strong, strong enough to resist him. But to stay on the safe side, don't let him put you into a trance. Don't take any drugs he offers you."

"I won't," I promised."

"It won't be easy. You'll have to pretend to go along with his plans, at least at first. I'll go to the meeting tonight. I'll convince Chuck and Sergeant Baker to come, too."

"Okay," I said, totally disappointed. I was counting on Lucinda to come up with a plan.

"We'll be on call if you need us. And let me know the minute Lucy learns anything regarding the location of that barn."

"Will do."

I watched some TV, then logged on to my computer. Before I knew it, Aunt Mary was calling me to come downstairs for lunch.

She'd put out a nice spread: cold pasta salad, crisp southern fried chicken, and ice cream for dessert. I surprised myself by eating quite a lot. When I finished, I looked up and discovered she was watching me, a frightened expression on her face.

She held out a pill. "Your Uncle Raymond wants me to give you this. He suggested that I put it in your food, but I couldn't, Simon."

I stared at her. "He's evil, Aunt Mary. Flush it down the toilet."

She nodded and went to do it.

"I'm going out," I said when she returned to the kitchen.

"But you mustn't!" Aunt Mary looked as though she were about to cry. "Your Uncle Raymond will be furious to find you gone. He told me to tell you to stay here."

"And he expected the pill would make me sleepy."

Her face flushed red. She nodded.

I flung myself out the door. Too full to run, I walked quickly to Lucinda's house. My cell phone rang.

"Hi, Simon," Pol said. "Why didn't you come to camp today?"

"I couldn't."

"Are you all right?"

"Not really. Lucy still can't tell us where she is. She said someone named Romie is guarding her."

"Romie?" Pol sounded excited. "Romie is Craig's wife. Her name's Ramona."

I let loose a sound of disgust. "Now why aren't I surprised? Listen, Pol, my uncle's planning something and it's connected to the meeting tonight. Please don't go!"

"I have to. They're expecting a poor turnout. People figure since your uncle's changed his mind about the playing fields, they might as well stay home and watch TV." Pol sighed. "Andy started it all. I can't let my brother down."

"I know, but—"

"You're going, aren't you?"

"I don't know. My uncle tried to drug me twice today. I've no idea where I'll be, come eight o'clock."

"Oh, Simon, I wish I could help. I want to be there for you until this awful time is over."

I gripped the cell phone till my knuckles turned white. "You are there for me, Pol. It helps. More than you know."

I changed my mind about visiting Lucinda and headed for the library. I sprawled out on one of the outdoor benches, but was too pent up to remain still. My thoughts bounced off each other like bumper cars. I couldn't come up with a solution, only the determination to save Lucy and myself from Raymond's clutches, and that was proving harder and harder to do.

I took off running and ended up in a park, where I drank what seemed like gallons of water from the fountain. I wandered through town, counted the minutes that passed, knowing each one brought Lucy and me closer to our doom. I jogged back to the library and fell asleep on the same bench I'd sat on earlier in the day.

"Simon, it's me."

"What's up, Lucy?"

"Romie took a slat off the window. The barn is blue!"

"That's great! Is it navy blue? Bright blue?"

"Bright blue. There are trees all around it, as far as I can see. Does that help?"

My excitement shot through with my message. "I think so, since most barns are red or white." I grinned. "I'll let our Great-Aunt Lucinda know. She'll send the news along."

"Do you think I'll get out of here today? I want to be with you, Simon."

"I hope today will be the day." My sense of impending danger made me add, "I have a feeling it will soon be over."

"Good. I can't wait to leave this place."

A minute later I was relating everything to Lucinda.

"I know where that barn is! I'll call Chuck. He and Sergeant Baker will get her."

I glanced down at my watch. How did it get to be five o'clock so fast? "How long will it take them to drive out there?" '

"About twenty minutes," Lucinda said. "I'll have them bring her to my house. If all goes well, you'll be seeing your sister in less than an hour."

Chapter Twenty-Seven

I was so busy talking to Lucinda, I never heard the two men come at me from behind. They flanked me on both sides. Each grabbed an upper arm and dragged me to a black car hidden behind bushes, only twenty feet from where I'd been sitting.

Frantically, I tried to shake free. This was a public place. Where was everyone? Anyone? I swung my head from side to side, but no one was in sight. Of course these goons would have made certain of that. When I opened my mouth to yell, a huge hand clamped over half my face. One of the men pushed my head down so I could climb into the back seat of the car. I kicked him in the shins. He swore softly and clouted me on the head.

"Ow!"

The guy was about to hit me again, when the other thug shook his head.

"Easy does it," he ordered. His voice had a harsh accent. Russian, I decided. "The boss said to handle him with kid gloves."

The guy who hit me said something back in Russian. Then he shoved me onto the seat and got in next to me.

I scrambled along the seat and yanked on the door lever. It wasn't locked! I opened the door and jumped out. Maybe I could get away! Maybe—

Before I took a step, the Russian who'd hit me was ramming me back inside the car. "Stay here and act good," he said in accented English, "or you'll be sorry."

The other guy revved the motor and we sped down the path meant for pedestrians. I stared out the window, waving frantically at the few people we passed. No one seemed to notice.

I felt a sting and looked down at my arm. The thug was jabbing me with a hypodermic needle. I struggled to shake free, but the creep was too strong.

The driver turned around, a pirate's grin on his ugly mug. "Good job, Ivan. That will keep him quiet for the next three hours."

I tried every trick I knew to remain conscious, but whatever narcotic they'd given me took immediate effect. Vivid images crossed my mind—a howling black dog, a little girl running, an old woman shouting.

Lucinda! I need you! I blinked furiously, determined to stay alert so I could see where they were taking me, but my eyes clamped shut. The car's motor hummed in harmony with the effects of the drug, lulling me to sleep.

I must stay awake! I closed my mind, but it was no defense against the drug's numbing power. I couldn't even wiggle a finger. I was paralyzed! Terror shot through my body. Was this how I'd be—comatose and immobile—after Raymond took over my body and my brain? Where would *I* be? Would I still be conscious, watching and suffering?

I felt a panic attack coming on, and was almost relieved when the narcotic numbed my anxiety. I remained barely conscious. *I must stay awake! I must stay awake!* Thoughts drifted into my head and floated away like puffy, white clouds on a sunny day.

The car stopped. I felt myself being dragged down stairs. The men cursed as they tripped and stumbled. A light flared. My eyes fluttered open. I closed them quickly when I caught one of the men eyeing me. But I'd managed to see the floor. Linoleum. A dank odor filled my nostrils. I was in a basement. I heard the gurgling of a water cooler, and I knew where I was! In the basement of Town Hall.

A spasm of terror worse than the earlier one had me quivering with fear. My uncle was planning to hold his transformation right here. Somehow it was connected to the meeting about the playing fields!

"Simon, help me! I don't know where I am!" Lucy's words filled my head. She was crying.

I had no idea what she was talking about. Had Raymond ordered his men to move her? I wanted to calm her down but couldn't form the words, not even in my mind.

"Why don't you answer me?" Lucy demanded between sobs. "I don't want them to come after me! Tell me where to go so they won't find me."

I struggled to understand what she was saying. Did she think Chuck and Sergeant Baker were more of Raymond's henchmen? Had she run away from them and gotten lost somewhere? Somewhere out in farm country with darkness coming on?

"Simon!" Lucy pleaded. "Tell me what to do! I can't run any more."

Maybe the two goons who'd grabbed me were after her now. I knew what fate was in store for Lucy! My poor sister was going to be Raymond's victim, like those other little girls he'd had killed.

Tears spilled down my face. No one could stop my uncle from carrying out his diabolical plans. Here I was, lying drugged in the basement of Town Hall as helpless as a baby, because I'd been careless every step of the way. My uncle had told me the transformation would take place this evening. I was so used to wandering around town and going where I liked, I had a false sense of freedom. I should have figured he'd send men out to get me when he was ready.

I'd been a fool to listen to Lucinda, a batty old woman with no common sense! If she had any, she'd have advised me to run fast and far from Buckley after that first infusion. My uncle was clever. He had money, clout, and ruthless assassins to carry out his orders. What chance had I, a fifteen-year-old kid, to save Lucy and myself?

I lost consciousness—for how long I had no idea—when Lucinda came through loud and clear, jolting me awake.

"Simon, answer me this minute! Let me know you're all right? Don't tell me that devil has you in his clutches!"

My aunt's fear and anger ricocheted inside my head. It took me a minute or two to get my thoughts in order.

"He had two men grab me and drug me. I think it's wearing off."

"Where are you?'

"In the basement of Town Hall."

"Town hall?" After a pause, she asked, "where they're holding the meeting tonight?"

"Yes. There's something else. Something important. Can't remember what it is."

"That nephew of mine is planning something awful. Simon, get out of there right now!"

"As soon as I can. Lucy contacted me. She's lost. I was too weak to answer her."

"That's terrible!" Lucinda sounded frantic. "Chuck and Jack Baker went looking for her. The barn was empty. No one was there."

"I don't know where she is. She sounded frightened. She was afraid some men would find her. Do you think she meant Chuck and Sergeant Baker? Or the men who brought me here?"

"I've no idea. We must find her and keep her safe. You need to get the hell out of there!"

Her anxiety came through, along with her words. I moved my legs. They felt tingly, but I was pretty sure they could support my weight. "I think I can walk now. Where shall I meet you?"

"Contact Lucy. T ake her someplace—anywhere— far from that building! I'll meet you after the town meeting."

"But Lucinda—"

She cut me off. "I've no time to explain, Simon. I must attend that meeting and counteract Raymond's wickedness."

She was gone. I shook my head in frustration. If I left the building, Raymond couldn't perform the transformation. Lucinda seemed to think he was planning something else, something diabolical, but I had no time to figure out what it could be. The drug was wearing off, but I still felt woozy. I could focus on only one thing at a time. I had to leave Town Hall before those goons returned and look for Lucy.

Walking took more effort than I'd expected. I stepped cautiously toward the steps, holding on to the wall for support. I glanced down at my watch. It was ten past eight. I'd been out longer than I realized. The special meeting was under way. My heart filled with hope as I started up the stairs. My uncle wouldn't dare harm me with half of Buckley looking on! Now the only obstacle was opening the door, which was probably locked.

I blinked as a bright light shone down on my face. I put up my arm to shield my eyes.

Craig's deep laughter boomed out. "And where do you think you're going?"

He aimed the flashlight at my eyes, forcing me back down the stairs. Biting back my disappointment, I noted for the first time the various pieces of furniture and other household objects scattered about the basement.

Craig thrust his chin toward a kitchen chair beside a coffee table covered with dishes and a bottle.

"Sit there and behave yourself until your uncle's ready for you." He sent me a smile of triumph. "Ten minutes more, and I won't have to deal with the likes of you ever again."

I had ten minutes to escape! My sense of self-preservation overcame my fear. I studied the gloating figure before me. I had little chance of beating him in a fight. Still, there were other ways of defeating one's enemy, especially an overconfident enemy certain he'd already won.

I glared at Craig. "Why are you so willing to do my uncle's dirty work?"

"The money's good."

"How good?" I asked like I was really interested, while my hands curled into fists. How I wanted to smash in that traitorous, boastful face!

"Let's see—I handled three 'incidents' recently at $500,000 a pop. I've made a million and a half since school let out."

I couldn't contain my outrage. "You got all that money for killing little girls! And one of them was your own camper."

Craig nodded. "Poor Melissa. She was a sweet child."

I opened my mouth to insult Craig, then decided on a different tack. Was this deviousness something I'd "inherited" from my uncle? At this point, I didn't care. I was grateful for the weapon and only hoped it worked.

"Tell me," I said softly, "is it for the money or because you hate kids? A teacher who kills kids is worse than a sexual predator."

Craig loomed over me with his fist jerked back, ready to strike. "Shut your mouth! You know nothing about it."

Bingo! I forced myself not to flinch, and took note of the bottle on the table beside me. "Why don't you explain so I'll understand."

My calm tone took the edge off his anger. "I had a son, Lionel. He was three when he caught meningitis. He died the next day. A donor's life force would have saved his life."

I gave a mirthless laugh. "A *'donor's life force'*? That's some spin you're putting on murder."

Craig didn't seem to hear me. "I swore I'd never have another child unless I'd be able to save his life. Your uncle promised to show me how to do it if I helped him with his transformation."

I stretched out my legs. Craig stepped back to give me more room, a sign he'd let down his guard. "And you believe my uncle will tell you how to do this? You trust him to keep his word?"

Craig took offense. "Of course. Why shouldn't I?"

"Because Raymond Davenport's a sneaking, conniving piece of garbage who thinks only of himself."

"He swore on a bible he'd teach me how to siphon the life force of donors."

Donors! Hah! I shook my head in disbelief. "You're so trusting. So naïve. Did you ever see him infuse anyone beside himself with another person's life force?"

"No, but he said it can be done."

"Well, it can't be done because you're not a Davenport." I laughed. "You let Raymond make a monkey out of you!"

Craig reached down to smack my face. I grabbed the bottle and smashed it against his skull. He fell to the floor with a thud.

I raced up the stairs, praying that Craig had left the door unlocked. As I approached the top step, I heard someone fumbling with the lock. I sped back down to the basement, and crouched behind a bookcase.

Raymond slowly descended the stairs. I held my breath. This was it! My only chance to escape was before me. I had to slip through the basement door my uncle had left ajar, and make it past the two men who were upstairs somewhere.

"Craig, what the hell are you doing on the floor?" Raymond demanded. He looked around the dimly lit basement. "Where's Simon?"

Craig held his head as he stumbled to his knees, and fell into the chair I'd been sitting in a minute ago. "He hit me on the head."

"You idiot! Don't tell me you let him get away!"

"He's down here somewhere. Unless he knows how to disappear into thin air."

Raymond gave a sigh of exasperation. "Spare me the jokes. I ask you to do one simple thing—keep my nephew in order until I need him—and you screw up. Just like your wife screwed up looking after my niece."

"I'm sorry about that, Raymond."

"Now I'll have to do the transformation without her."

"Is everything in order upstairs?" Craig asked.

Raymond didn't answer. He strode over to the wall and switched on the overhead lights. As he walked back toward Craig, he pulled two items from his back pocket. One was a dart. The other appeared to be a wide plastic straw. I covered my mouth to keep from making a sound.

"I believe you've worn out your usefulness. Thank you for everything, Craig. You and your worthless wife."

My mouth fell open as Craig huddled in the chair, a whimpering pool of terrified jelly.

"Please, Raymond. I'll do anything you want. Don't kill me. Don't—"

The dart struck Craig's forehead, and he crumpled to the ground. His gasps sounded like air being forced from a balloon. Raymond placed one end of the plastic tube into Craig's mouth, the other end into his own. When he removed it minutes later, sparks of charged energy danced in the air.

Run up the stairs and out the building! The words jangled in my brain, but I couldn't move. The shock of what I'd just witnessed had paralyzed me as effectively as the drug had earlier.

Raymond danced around the basement like the Energized Bunny. It would have been hilarious, watching my klutzy uncle jump and hop about, if Craig weren't lying dead a few feet away. I tensed as he circled the room, peering behind bureaus and armoires.

"Where are you, Simon?" he called out in a singsong voice. "Uncle Raymond's ready for you now."

I huddled behind the bookcase, trying to stop the tremors. Raymond opened an armoire in the far corner of the basement. If I wanted to live, I had to move! *Run across the floor. Up the stairs. Past the door standing ajar!*

Go now or he'll get you and do worse than he did to Craig!

But my feet remained glued to the floor.

Chapter Twenty-Eight

"Simon, I'm scared! This weird old lady's staring at me. She must be one of them!"

"Lucy?" Silently, I berated myself. These last few minutes I'd closed off communication with my sister and Lucinda.

"She's coming closer! Where are you?"

Raymond was coming closer. "Does she have white hair?"

"Yes. She looks like a witch!"

"She's our great-aunt Lucinda. Go with her. Do as she says."

"Are you sure?"

"Absolutely."

Too late, I remembered Lucinda's intention of coming to the meeting. I was about to tell Lucy not to enter Town Hall when my uncle grabbed me roughly by the shoulder. Craig's life force had made him fit and strong.

"Show time," Raymond said, laughing as though he'd said something amusing. He shoved me toward the stairs.

"Go on up, and no funny business."

I had no choice but to obey. I climbed the stairs and pushed open the door that might have led to my freedom, then realized my escape plan would never have worked. My uncle's two goons stood facing one another, their faces devoid of all expression. Raymond whispered to the leader, and they went down to the basement.

I gasped at the horrific scene before me. The thirty or so townspeople who had come to the meeting lay sprawled on the ground or slumped in chairs. They appeared to be unconscious or dead. A long table set along a side wall held an array of refreshments—cakes, cookies, pastries, iced tea, iced coffee, and pitchers of soda and lemonade.

I glared at my uncle. "What did you do, poison them?"

"Certainly not." Raymond laughed. "They're merely sedated. Resting before they help make our transformation a reality."

I recognized many of the people who had been caught in my uncle's trap. I stepped over them to get to Andy and his dad. *Where was Pol?*

"Andy, wake up!" I shook his shoulder, but he didn't so much as open an eye.

Raymond yanked me to my feet. "Don't waste any more of my time. I promise you, your friend won't suffer."

I shook my head in disbelief. "You'd kill all these people for an experiment?"

He frowned. "The transformation will work, Gregory, as you'll learn in a matter of minutes. Now be a good lad and sit quietly while I get everything ready for the big moment."

He escorted me to the small room across the hall and tied me to a chair. He left the door open so he could keep an eye on me as he went about his gruesome business. The two goons came up the basement stairs carrying Craig's body, which they'd covered with a blanket. Raymond gave them instructions, and they left the building through a rear door. I wondered if they'd be coming back inside or standing guard outside?

Where was Lucinda? Surely, she wouldn't bring Lucy into this hellhole. Where was Chuck? Sergeant Baker? I hadn't seen them or Pol among the unconscious bodies. She must have taken my advice and decided not to attend the meeting. But Andy and his father were going to die.

"Simon, where are you? I have Lucy."

"Lucinda!" I all but shouted her name aloud. "I'm still in Town Hall. Everyone here is unconscious. I think Raymond put something in the food and drinks to knock them out. He's about to start the transformation."

"Is he alone?"

"Right now he is. He killed Craig and took his life force, so he's strong. And he has two men. They carried Craig's body out back."

"Yes, I see them. They're loading it onto a pickup truck. Now listen to me, Simon, and do what I say if you want to get out of there alive."

"But Lucy—"

"Don't worry about Lucy. She's a good girl and she'll help."

"No! Leave Lucy out of this!"

"Can you see what Raymond's up to?"

"Kind of. He's tied me to a chair, but I think I can work myself free."

"Good! Your job is to tell me exactly what he's doing." She gave a snort. "I won't be able to answer since I'll be busy putting his gorillas out of commission."

"You can do that?" I asked, amazed.

"I'm a Davenport, aren't I? Quick, tell me what he's doing."

Still tied to the chair, I edged to the doorway and peered across the hall into the meeting hall. "He's going from person to person with that plastic tube-like thing."

"Get yourself loose and stop him! Break his concentration! Disrupt him any way you can. I'll be with you as soon I'm done."

"What about Lucy?" I asked, but Lucinda didn't answer.

I tugged at the cord that bound my hands, then decided I'd have better luck if I worked at loosening the knots with my fingers. The cord was thick and not that difficult to undo. Once my hands were free, I untied my feet and dashed across to the meeting hall where Raymondcrouched on the floor beside Andy.

"No!" I shouted as my uncle placed the plastic cylinder in my friend's mouth.

"Keep away, Gregory!" Raymond ordered, not pausing in his monstrous work.

I rushed at him and knocked the cylinder from his hand. Raymond cursed. He tried to hit me, but I'd already rolled out of reach and was shaking Mr. Coltrane's shoulder.

"Get up, Mr. C.! You have to wake up!"

Mr. Coltrane stirred and turned on his side. I was starting to feel we had a chance to make things right. Maybe Lucinda and I could save everyone, after all.

I slapped Andy's cheeks. "Wake up, dude!" Andy was such a glutton, he must have eaten like a pig and ingested a large dose of the sedative. He lay as still as a corpse. Frantic, I slapped him harder.

"Ouch!" I yelped. I stared up at Raymond, who had just walloped the side of my head. Catching me off guard, he twisted my arm behind my back. I was furious at myself for letting him get the drop on me.

"Save your heroics! They're all goners." Raymond shouted, his face contorted with rage. "Now keep out of my way. I must get them ready. The transformation depends on harvesting the life force of all of them within thirty minutes."

"There won't be any transformation!" I said through the pain spreading across my shoulder.

"Don't be stupid! I'll be inhabiting your body and your mind in less than an hour!"

Never releasing his brutal grip, Raymond yanked me to my feet and pushed me forward. I had to step over unconscious bodies. "Back you go while I finish my work! This time I'll tie those knots tighter."

I *had* to stall for time. I pretended to trip and fell to my knees, which earned me another painful arm jerk. *Don't try to fight him. Be wily. Outwit him.*

I forced myself to speak calmly. "You're going to break my arm. I don't think you want to do that."

My uncle released his grip. "Of course I don't." With surprising gentleness, he turn me around so that we faced one another. The smile he gave me was warm. Loving. "Ah Gregory, if only you'd cooperate, this would be a wonderful bonding experience for us both."

Not for me, it wouldn't! As we walked across the hall, I marveled at my stupidity. For a kid who aced all his tests, I'd been awfully slow not to have picked up the obvious: Raymond was bonkers. A madman.

Crazy calls for acting crazy. "Uncle Raymond?" I said, making my voice waver.

"Hmm?" He sat me down in the chair and reached for the rope.

"Will it hurt?"

Raymond's smile was gentle, but his eyes were burning coals. My stomach lurched. "I imagine you'll feel something of a shock. Then nothing."

"Will I still be conscious of things?"

I tried not to flinch when he patted my shoulder. "Perhaps. But don't worry. I'll take good care of you."

I stiffened my arms to keep from pushing him away. "I won't fight you any more. I'll sit here quietly while you do what you have to."

"Good, Gregory." He dropped the rope, but this time he closed the door behind him.

I called to Lucinda, but she didn't answer. Should I return to the hall and surprise Raymond? Bad idea. I couldn't possibly wake up everyone by myself. He'd only tie me up, and I'd be a sitting guinea pig with no chance of escaping his transformation.

"Lucinda!" I tried again, louder this time.

"Did it!" she announced, clearly pleased with herself. "Those two are down for the count, and I don't see any more of them in the area. Are you all right?"

"For the moment. Raymond's gone back to preparing those poor unconscious people for their part in the Great Transformation."

"So he thinks. Lucy and I are coming in. You, me, and Lucy are going to create a force field around Raymond and sap him of his power."

"A force field?" My anxiety rose to a new level. "I've never done anything like that before. And Lucy—"

"Your sister's quite a girl," Lucinda said proudly. "A real Davenport. She's as strong as you are. If a nine-year-old can help save a bunch of strangers from death and her brother from a transformation, then you can do your part without squawking."

She'd managed to shut me up. "All right. What do I do?"

The way Lucinda explained it, it was like hooking up a three-way conference call. I was to concentrate on exerting my energy to form a force field with Lucy and Lucinda, which would deplete Raymond of his powers and newly-acquired strength. Lucinda deflected every question I came up with, insisting I wasn't to worry. She would direct the force field.

I felt like I was about to take a final exam weeks before the scheduled date. "But Lucinda, what if he turns that force back on us?"

"It's now or never, Simon. Keep in mind that we are three and he is one. Here we come!"

I opened the door and crossed the hall. Raymond was moving feverishly from one prone body to another. I swallowed a lump of fear when I saw he'd inserted a plastic tube into each of their mouths. He'd placed an enormous mirror against the table holding the tainted food and drink. What role did a mirror play in his plan?

Raymond mumbled to himself as he worked. He didn't appear to have heard me circle around to his right. But he looked up when Lucinda and Lucy walked through the front door.

"Damn you, Lucinda! I might have known you'd interfere with my project." Raymond stepped toward Lucy, his arm outstretched. The smile plastered on his face was more gruesome than a fright mask. "But thanks for delivering Lucy. Your timing's perfect."

Lucinda's eyes glittered as she glared at her nephew. "You won't harm this child or anyone else!"

I ran at Raymond, knocking him down with a head butt. "Don't you touch her, you monster!"

Raymond got to his feet and continued walking toward Lucy. I lowered my head to tackle him again, when Lucinda silently instructed me to stand where I was. "You must remain calm for the force field to work. We begin now!"

A surge of power nearly knocked me off my feet as Lucy and Lucinda's energy joined mine.

"Visualize a wall of fire surrounding Raymond," Lucinda ordered.

I did as instructed and gasped as a ring of red fire encircled my uncle.

"We are three and he is one," we silently chanted. The fire turned blue then to pure violet energy.

Raymond froze. He stared at Lucinda in shock.

She laughed. "Your uncle didn't know the extent of my power," she silently told Lucy and me. "Get ready when he retaliates."

"I'm scared," Lucy mumbled. Her face crumpled, a sure sign she was about to cry.

"We'll beat him, Lucy," Lucinda said. "But we must stay connected. Focus on the force field."

I bent over double when a powerful gale wind twisted like a tornado inside my head, set on breaking my connection with Lucy and Lucinda. I felt Lucy letting go.

"Lucy!" I cried.

She fell to the ground, hugging herself.

"Lucy, get up and join your brother and me," Lucinda instructed. "Your uncle can't harm us. We are three and he is one. Say it!"

Lucy sniffed.

"Say it!" Lucinda ordered. "We are three and he is one."

"We are three and he is one!" We repeated it again and again. I watched Raymond lower his head and fold in on himself as he were bowing to our combined force.

But he was only gathering strength. This time, his retaliation was powerful enough to break our connections with one another. We stumbled backward. A massive electrical shock knocked me to the ground. I felt ill when I caught a glimpse of what was running through Raymond's mind: killing Lucinda, draining Lucy's life force, and transforming himself into my body.

"He's stronger than you thought," I told Lucinda.

"He imbibed some of the life force of these people as he was preparing them for his transformation."

"What should we do? He's coming toward Lucy."

"We do it again. This time imagine the wall of fire seven feet tall. Taller than Raymond. Ready, Lucy?"

Lucy shook her head. "I can't."

I concentrated on visualizing a wall of fire. It was high but didn't blaze nearly as well as the one the three of us had created. We managed to subdue Raymond until he gathered up enough strength to fight back. We'd reached an impasse.

How much longer could we hold him? Lucinda was tiring. Despite her powers, she was an old woman, and she'd already subdued those two thugs outside.

Lucy was crying softly. "Come on, Luce," I begged. "You have to help us."

"I can't."

"Yes, you can. We need you. Your force will make the difference."

Lucy shook her head.

I grew desperate. "Awful things will happen if you don't help us now. We'll never be together again."

"Lucy, come to me, my little angel," Raymond coaxed, crooking a finger to my sister.

"He's a murderer, Lucy! He killed our parents!"

Lucy gave a start as if she were awakening from a dream. I stared in amazement at the current of air swirling around her. Oh no! Was this another of Raymond's tricks?

I relaxed when I saw the huge grin on Lucinda's face. "Good girl! I knew you had it in you."

The whirlwind spun faster and faster. Lucy stretched out her arms. An awesome surge of energy coursed through us when we joined hands. I'd never imagined my little sister was this powerful.

"We are three and he is one!" we chanted as our force field, now a brilliant white, encircled Raymond. He turned one way, then another, but found no escape.

He opened his mouth and gasped for air. A strangled cry rose from his throat.

"The life force he's taken in is backfiring. He's choking," Lucinda explained.

"Will he die?" I asked, though I already knew the answer.

The air became still. We stared at the body lying on the ground.

I ran to Lucy and held her in a fierce hug. "We did it, Gretel! We defeated the witch!"

"Only this witch was a man."

Lucinda tapped me on the shoulder. "We have to wake everyone up. Make sure they're all right."

"Of course." I paused, thinking I'd heard a siren. "Did someone call the police?"

Lucinda grinned. "I believe your friend Pol did. I told her to give us twenty minutes then to call Sergeant Baker."

Epilogue

The first Saturday in November, Lucy, Aunt Mary, Lucinda, and I sat around Aunt Mary's kitchen table—the only piece of furniture she'd brought from her old house—to discuss our first Thanksgiving in our new home.

"I don't want to invite Aunt Grace," I said. "She wasn't very nice to me."

Aunt Mary gave me one of her adoring but exasperated looks. "Try to be more forgiving. Grace acted out of concern for Lucy. She didn't want your uncle to find out where they were living."

"And when you disobeyed her and visited Lucy, her worst fears came true," Aunt Lucinda chimed in.

"I don't need the two of you ganging up on me," I said.

"Aunt Grace was mostly nice," Lucy said. "And I know she loves you, Simon."

"She has some way of showing it," I grumbled.

Aunt Mary held up her pen. "Shall we invite Grace or not?"

I shrugged. "Whatever. With three against one, what does it matter what I want?"

Lucinda winked. "Of course your wishes matter. You're the only male in our family. But when it comes to a vote, adults have more clout."

Is that what we are? A family? As though to answer my question, Lucy crept into Aunt Mary's lap and shifted about until she was comfortable. Aunt Mary kissed the top of her head. Interesting, how Lucy and Aunt Mary had taken to one another.

"Oh, all right," I said. "She can come."

"Grace is a 'yes,'" Aunt Mary said, writing in her notepad.

"I thought we'd invite my former neighbor, Martha Barrister," Lucinda said. "She took good care of me after Craig put me in the hospital."

I cleared my throat. "Pol and Andy will be having dinner with their family, but I asked them to stop by for dessert."

Lucy giggled. "We'd better buy three extra pies for Andy."

"I'll bake brownies," Lucinda said. "Andy loves my brownies."

"And your apple crumb cake, please, Aunt Lucinda," Lucy said

I withdrew into myself and let their conversation drift over me like a breeze. I didn't know why I'd made such a fuss about inviting Aunt Grace to Thanksgiving dinner. I really didn't care if she came or not. Besides, she was probably in Europe.

I *was* glad Lucy and I had a home at last, with the two adults I loved the most in the world. But ever since things had settled down, I felt trapped most of the time. My aunts came up with a bunch of rules and regulations I was supposed to follow. Which was a laugh after all I'd gone through.

I never knew when my mind would flash back to that horrific scene in Town Hall. Lucinda and I had been able to save everyone except an elderly man. For everyone's sake, Raymond and Craig's deaths were recorded as heart attacks, though the police knew my uncle had killed Craig and had drugged the refreshments. I only told Pol, Andy, and Chuck the entire story, though I imagined it would eventually get out to more people .

I didn't care if it did or not. Raymond and Craig were dead, and the two goons were in jail on kidnapping charges. Now, if only I could relax and get on with my life.

The doorbell rang. Lucy ran to answer it. She skipped back into the room, followed by Pol. "Pol's here," she announced unnecessarily.

Pol greeted everyone and placed a shopping bag on the table. "Mom sent over a lasagna and a salad. She figures you haven't finished unpacking all the kitchen stuff yet. Shall I put them in the refrigerator?"

"Yes, dear," Aunt Mary said. "Please thank your mother for us. She's been very kind to us."

Lucinda grinned. "I think we were very lucky to have found a house half a block from the Coltrane family. Don't you agree, Simon?"

"Mmmm. Ready to go?" I asked Pol.

She flashed me an understanding smile. "Sure."

"I'll get my jacket."

As I opened the hall closet, I heard Pol asking how we liked our new home.

"It will be lovely, once the workmen fix the leak in the upstairs bathroom and the heating system," Aunt Mary said.

"I see you've still plenty of boxes to unpack," Pol said as I rejoined everyone in the kitchen.

"We'll get it done," Lucinda said. "All in good time."

I took Pol's hand and led her outside. As soon as the door slammed shut, I took her in my arms for a long kiss. Then we clasped hands and started walking.

"What's wrong?" Pol asked.

I shrugged. "Nothing."

"Maybe you have a problem living so close to me."

I squeezed her hand. "That's the part I like."

"Then what is it?"

I stopped walking. "I'm glad Lucy and I have a home and Lucinda's our guardian. But it's so weird, living with both my aunts."

Pol scrunched up her face. I could tell she was totally confused. "I thought you liked your aunts."

"I love them dearly, but now that Raymond's not around, Aunt Mary can be downright bossy. She makes up lists of chores for me to do, and worries that I'm spending too much time on my computer .

"And Lucinda! Not a day passes when she doesn't ask if I did my homework. She wants to know the grade of every test and quiz I take because, after all, I have to get into a good college. I tell her she doesn't have to worry. I'm in Honors Classes and I have a high average. In that case I won't bug you, she says, but the questions start up again the next day."

I caught my breath and continued. "I thought it was great when Lucinda suggested we all live together. But I never expected my two aunts would get so chummy. That they'd gang up against me like— like—"

"Like concerned parents," Pol said.

"They're not my parents!" I snapped.

We walked in silence. I didn't need extra-powerful senses to know I'd hurt Pol's feelings.

"Sorry," I muttered.

"Lucinda and Mary are your family. They love you, Simon."

We turned the corner and headed for the library. I had to tell Pol what was on my mind, even though it was kooky, bizarre, and totally nuts.

"Look, I'm glad Raymond's gone. He was evil through and through, and he deserved to die, but—"

I felt Pol's concern as she walked beside me.

I drew a deep breath. "But I had all this freedom. I did what I wanted, went where I felt like going. But now they keep tags on me: where are you going? What time will you be home? Call if you're out after eleven o'clock. Jeez!"

"Wow!" she said in mock astonishment. "They treat you like an ordinary sixteen-year-old kid."

"Right! After all I've been through, how can I be an ordinary kid?"

Pol giggled as she wrapped her arms around my waist. "I know you're not ordinary. So do they. They're trying to make your life and Lucy's as normal as possible."

"But they have all these dumb rules," I insisted. "And they're so—intrusive."

"I can imagine."

"I mean, I saved people's lives!"

"My father and brother's included, for which I'm eternally grateful. But now your uncle's gone and life goes on. Kind of like it's supposed to."

Kind of like it's supposed to. The library came into view.

"Thanks," I said.

Pol fixed her sparkling blue-green eyes on mine. "For what?"

"For understanding. For making me understand."

"Oh. Okay."

"Want to go inside, take out a few books?"

"Sure. Why not?"

As the mechanical glass doors opened, she asked, "how about going to the movies tonight? Andy asked Gilda Morrison out, and I know he'd like us to double with them."

I felt wounded. "He asked Gilda out and never told me!"

Pol's eyebrows shot up. "How could he? You haven't been available lately."

Pol was right. I'd been moody and withdrawn, except with her. All the bad stuff with Raymond had delayed my mourning for my parents and my old life.

And now I had a new life. I was still adjusting to the awful things my uncle had done. But I had Lucy, I had Pol. I had my aunts and Andy and other new friends at school. I had my future and so much to be thankful for.

I leaned over and kissed Pol lightly on the lips. "Text Andy. Tell him we'll double with him tonight."

Pol grinned. "I already did."

About the Author

A former Spanish teacher, Marilyn Levinson writes mysteries, romantic suspense and novels for kids. Her books have received many accolades. As Allison Brook she writes the Haunted Library series. *Death Overdue*, the first in the series, was an Agatha nominee for Best Contemporary Novel in 2018. *Out of Circulation*, the eighth book in the series, will be published in August, 2024. Other mysteries include the Golden Age of Mystery Book Club series and the Twin Lakes series.

Her juvenile novel, *And Don't Bring Jeremy* was a nominee for six state awards. *Rufus and Magic Run Amok* was an International Reading Association-Children's Book Council Children's Choice and has recently come out in a new edition as the first in a series of four books. *Rufus and the Witch's Drudge*, the second in the series, will be published in 2024.

Marilyn lives on Long Island, where many of her books take place. She loves traveling, reading, doing crossword puzzles and Sudoku, chatting on FaceTime with her grandkids and playing with her kittens,

Romeo and Juliet.

SOCIAL MEDIA HANDLES:
Facebook: https://www.facebook.com/marilyn.levinson.10?ref=ts&fref=ts
Goodreads: https://www.goodreads.com/author/show/161602.Marilyn_Levinson
Twitter: https://twitter.com/MarilynLevinson ; https://twitter.com/AllisonBrookML
BookBub: https://www.bookbub.com/authors/marilyn-levinson
Pinterest: http://www.pinterest.com/marilev/
Instagram: https://www.instagram.com/marilynlevinsonauthor/

AUTHOR WEBSITE:
http://www.marilynlevinson.com

Also by Marilyn Levinson

Middle Grade and YA:

And Don't Bring Jeremy
The Fourth-Grade Four
A Place to Start
No Boys Allowed
Rufus and Magic Run Amok
Rufus and the Witch's Drudge
Getting Back to Normal

For Adults:

A Murderer Among Us
Murder in the Air (Twin Lakes series)
Murder a la Christie
Murder the Tey Way (Golden Age of Mystery Book Club series)
Giving Up the Ghost
Dangerous Relations
The Haunted Library series written as Allison Brook (8 books)